THE SWALLOWS

THE SWALLOWS tells the story of a young country girl,
Germaine, who comes to Madame Severin's shop in answer
to an advertisement for an assistant. She mistakenly comes
to the shop next door which is run by Bertrand, Madame
Severin's nephew and his friend Fernand, and where the
stock may vary from broken china to motor cycles according
to the mood of the vague and disorganized young men. More
than this, however, THE SWALLOWS is an exposition of the
absurdities of our daily life, of the need for love and affection,
of the tragedy of growing old and of the continual desire for
the new and untried.

The play itself has had a chequered career. Acclaimed by
Parisian playwrights, Ionesco and Anouilh among them, it
had previously received indifferent reviews from the critics.
The play subsequently had a long run in Paris, in the
production of Arlette Reinerg, who also played the part of
Germaine.

Roland Dubillard was born in France, lives in Paris and is
in his forties. He was first known as an actor and cabaret
artist until THE SWALLOWS and his second play, THE
HOUSE OF BONES, were produced in Paris and highly
praised by leading Parisian dramatists. He has also written
a volume of poetry, which is in the process of being translated
into English. He belongs to no school of writing, either as
founder or follower, but, like Rimbaud with whom he has
much in common both in character and his work, he occupies
a unique position in modern European literature.

Barbara Wright has a deservedly high reputation as the
translator of the novels of Queneau and the plays of Arrabal
among other important works of modern French writing.

PLAYSCRIPT 16

'the swallows'

TRANSLATED BY BARBARA WRIGHT

roland dubillard

CALDER AND BOYARS · LONDON

Printed in Great Britain
by Latimer Trend Limited
Whitstable Kent

ABOUT THE PLAY

Les Naives Hirondelles was first performed at the Theatre de
Poche Montparnasse in Paris on 16th October 1961. The author
was unknown as a playwright, although he had had some success
as a music hall performer, under the name Gregoire, and the
critics were nearly all hostile. Then Andre Roussin went to see
it, and wrote enthusiastically to the press, praising the play
and bringing out aspects of it that the critics had overlooked.
Eugene Ionesco and other playwrights followed suite, and one
by one the critics returned, saw the play again and changed
their minds. The play had a long run and several revivals with
the same cast in Arlette Reinerg's production. It was seen for
a few performances only in a French season at the Piccadilly
Theatre at Easter 1965. By that time, M. Dubillard had been
given a leading place in the French avant-garde, especially
after the bitter-sweet Naives Hirondelles (the title of a song
that takes on a curious poignancy in the farcical comi-tragedy
of everyday life that distinguishes the play) was followed by
the death-obsessed La Maison d'Os (The House of Bones), which,
although less successful at the box office, was recognized as a
major modern drama by critics and other writers.

The Swallows had its first English performance at the Traverse
Theatre Club in Edinburgh during the 1966 Edinburgh Festival,
and subsequently an unsuccessful short run at the New Arts
Theatre Club in Britain. It was then recognized that there were
serious deficiencies in the translation, which has since been
extensively revised. Now that it has at last, after many delays,
been published, it should begin to have the same successful
career in Britain that it had in France after initial setbacks.
The Traverse production was produced by Ronald Taylor and
the cast included:

Ewen Solon	as	Fernand
Tim Preece	as	Bertrand
Tessa Wyatt	as	Germaine
Viola Keats	as	Mme Severin

The Swallows was first performed as Naives Hirondelles at
the Theatre de Poche Montparnasse, Paris on 16th October,
1961 with the following cast:

Tania Balachova	Madame Severin
Arlette Reinerg	Germaine
Gregoire	Fernand
Bernard Fresson	Bertrand

The play was directed by Arlette Reinerg

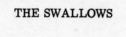

THE SWALLOWS

CHARACTERS

MADAME SEVERIN

GERMAINE

BERTRAND

FERNAND

ACT ONE

(The interior of a shop - though what it sells is not
readily apparent - one autumn evening. GERMAINE,
young, modest, unpretentious, comes in through the
street door. She looks nervously around her and
discovers that the shop is deserted)

GERMAINE. (Calling) Anyone there? (Aside) If this isn't
it, it won't be anywhere. (She sits down on her suit-
case) ... (Making her mind up) Anyway, this is it.
(Calling) Is this Madame Séverin's?... (Aside) Oh
well, so what, I'm going to stay here. They did
advertise, didn't they? So I shall stay. This makes
the eighth. The eighth I've been to... I've certainly
seen some shops. (Looking round) These people must
be just starting, too. The hats haven't come yet, they're
waiting for them. (Pause) Oh, I'm going. (Another
pause. Calling) Anyone there? Is this Madame Séverin's?
(Aside) The bbb... (Pause, then she says gently) Oh,
do come... (She goes off into a daydream, with staring
eyes, and finally murmurs) Auntie, Auntie, Auntie...
(She pulls herself together and looks at her surroundings.
Ironically) It isn't so bad here, eh... (Then, forgetting
her inhibitions, she sings out) Excuse me, excuse me...
(With some surprise she discovers in a corner) A tyre!
A tyre! I've come to the wrong shop again. It's not fair.
What about the advertisement, though? No hats... Not
one hat. Not a single hat!

(Enter a lady, hurriedly. She is MADAME SÉVERIN)

MME S. No one in?

GERMAINE. No.

MME S. Huh! You want to shout louder, then. (Shouting)
Anyone in? (Silence. To GERMAINE) Are you staying?

GERMAINE. Yes..., no..., yes, I'll wait.

MME S. Good. You can do me a favour, then: my bottle.
(She puts it down on the table) I must go: got to cook
for the men. Don't worry, dear, they'll be back soon.
Not very warm, is it? (On her way out) It's for a litre
of bleach, just in case. I'll be back, good evening.
(She's gone)

GERMAINE. Excuse me! Madame! Madame!... Is this
Madame Séverin's? (Aside) Ah well, I shall just make
myself at home, and anyway, so what? And at this
time of day...
Cook for the men?... A litre of bleach... Nothing but
people you don't know, what a bore. Well, anyway, they
can't send me back to Pontoise at this hour, can they?
No, really, there are limits.
It's quite true, though: you're looking for a job, they've
got one to offer, they think they're Napoleon. (She opens
a magazine. She yawns noisily) Cook for...

(Another short silence. Then a long string, one end of
which is by GERMAINE's feet, becomes taut; someone
in the next room has picked up the other end. This
someone enters. He walks slowly, because he's winding
up the string. He is also carrying a small enamel bowl
under his arm. His name is BERTRAND. GERMAINE
has stood up. The moment arrives when BERTRAND
notices GERMAINE)

I came, well, the thing is, why I came, good evening
Monsieur, I, because, I heard, I mean I read...

BERTRAND. Well, what do you know! Isn't that extraordinary!
Good evening, Mademoiselle. I recognized you at once.

GERMAINE. Oh no, surely not, Monsieur.

BERTRAND. Oh but I did. I was only thinking about you this

afternoon. Here! (He rummages among a pile of magazines and shows her a cover-girl) You see. You've been seen around these parts.

GERMAINE. That's not me.

BERTRAND. Really?... The light isn't very good here. Even so, you _are_ like her, aren't you?

GERMAINE. I don't know. Were you expecting this lady, then?

BERTRAND. Of course I wasn't. I don't know her. That's why I was so surprised.

GERMAINE. I'm terribly sorry.

BERTRAND. Don't be sorry. You're not so bad looking, either.

GERMAINE. I came, because, this morning, I read...

BERTRAND. Oh well, that's quite another matter then. I beg your pardon. What can I have the pleasure of selling you, Mademoiselle?

GERMAINE. ... in the paper... No: I came to see you because, well, it's like this: I've lost my aunt and I'm looking for a...

BERTRAND. I see! Well, perhaps it's just as well, because I must say there isn't very much at the moment. Good. Well then... though I rather think we're closed at this hour. What time is it?... Well, the thing is, yes: in the paper? That must have been Fernand again. Never mind; since you're here, you might as well sit down. I said: sit down - I'll be able to see you better.

(He examines her with the table lamp)

GERMAINE. You see, this morning. I was reading the paper, because I've just come from Pontoise. This _is_ where Madame Séverin lives, isn't it?

BERTRAND. Madame Séverin? Yes. Do you know her? Let me see your profile.

GERMAINE. No, I don't know her. It's that my aunt...

BERTRAND. Oh, you'll meet her. There's no difficulty about that. Good, well, that's fine. It's yes, so far as I'm concerned. (Calling) Fernand! Oh, the silly bugger. That's fine, don't get up, Mademoiselle. And in the meantime, what's your name? (Calling) Fernand! Hey!

GERMAINE. Germaine Tilbout.

BERTRAND. Tilbout... (Calling) Oy! Fernand! - Germaine? Right. Well, you'll have to see Fernand. I've got to go. But it'll be all right. When you see Fernand, just tell him to look at you. He probably won't understand why, because... but that doesn't matter. Tell him I'll explain later. And tell him it's not at all nice of him to have secrets from me. All the more so as it was my idea, he really might've.

GERMAINE. But when shall I see Madame Séverin?

BERTRAND. Any minute now. Very soon. You're lovely. Have you seen my hat? No, don't bother, if you haven't seen it it can't be here. (Calling) Fernand! Doesn't matter, he's bound to come soon.

(He goes out)

GERMAINE. (Left alone in the lamplight) More lunatics! (Stops talking, looks round) Or else it's wholesale millinery; oh no, not for me: the moment you finish one hat you're packing up dozens like it in a crate, instead of selling it. Making hats and not selling them, that's not my idea at all. All the trouble and none of the pleasure. What a bore! (Looking round again) ... Not one. Not a single one. And they're not in any great hurry, either. It's just as well that Auntie's dead, because... I might just as well have stayed in Pontoise, what do they think they're doing!

(FERNAND can be heard approaching. He's humming

'Simple Swallows')

GERMAINE. That'll be Fernand. Oh, I wish she'd come,
I'm scared.

(Enter FERNAND)

How do you do?...

FERNAND. Haha! we have company! Don't let me disturb
you. Have you by any chance seen a young man called
Bertrand?

GERMAINE. Oh, I don't know whether he was called Bertrand.

FERNAND. Yes, a tall chap, this high, with a hat... Well,
he's not really as tall as all that. You must have been
here when he was calling me: Fernand. I'm Fernand.

GERMAINE. Good evening, Monsieur. He went out. That
way.

FERNAND. Didn't he tell you to tell me something?

GERMAINE. He told me to tell you to look at me.

FERNAND. Oh, he's at it again!

GERMAINE. That's what I told him. I couldn't for the life
of me make out why he told me to tell you that.

FERNAND. It's always the same, with Bertrand. You have
to guess. Anyway, sit down and let me look at you.
(Humming) 'Winter has withered the flowers...' Ah,
you've come about the advertisement.

GERMAINE. Yes, Monsieur.

FERNAND. But why, why did he put in an advertisement?
Really, love, there are moments... Ah well, what's
done's done. I'll tell him, I'll say: in that case, you
needn't have bothered to ask _my_ opinion.

GERMAINE. I've just come from Pontoise, Monsieur.

FERNAND. Well, you don't think anyone's going to send you back to Pontoise, do you my pretty?

GERMAINE. My name's Germaine Tilbout.

FERNAND. Well, Germaine, sit down again. We'll have a little chat. Did Bertrand put that there?

(He points to a hammock on the table)

GERMAINE. I don't know, Monsieur.

FERNAND. My name's Monsieur Fort. You'd better start calling me Fernand, it'll save time. (He starts slinging the hammock) Well, Germaine. Can you mend china?

GERMAINE. No.

FERNAND. (Abashed) What d'you mean, no? You can't mend china?

GERMAINE. No. I've never had to.

FERNAND. (After a pause, calls) Bertrand! (More or less aside) I tell you, that fellow's unique. (To her) So you can't mend china. Fine, that's fine. There's something to be said for frankness, I suppose. Even so, though, even so. There's nothing difficult about breaking china, I'll admit that, but mending it, after all! (Doing his best) Maybe you're at least willing to learn?

GERMAINE. (Pale) I... I came about the... (She chokes)

FERNAND. Are you willing to learn?

GERMAINE. Me? But Monsieur, what a thing to ask! ... But Monsieur...

FERNAND. Willing or not willing?

GERMAINE. Perhaps... I might possibly... be willing...

FERNAND. Ah well, that's good enough. Now you've got up again? Oh go on, sit down. We've got all day.

14

GERMAINE. (Her last hope) Madame Séverin. I'd liked to have seen Madame Séverin.

FERNAND. I know her. You'll see her later on. She's my next-door neighbour, Madame Séverin. Now what...?

GERMAINE. It's just that I've come to the wrong shop.

FERNAND. Oh no. She sells hats.

GERMAINE. (Relieved) Ah! That's it. (She laughs)... You see, I'm a modiste! That's it! I've come to the wrong shop. Excuse me, Monsieur, I'm so sorry. I'll be going... I'm sorry, I just can't help it.

(She giggles)

FERNAND. Well, that's a good one! ... And she's going! Huh, that's very funny. She came to the wrong shop. What a girl! (Calling) Bertrand! Bertrand'll love that. Hurry up, it'll be shut. Goodbye, love. It's just one of those things.

(Enter MADAME SÉVERIN)

FERNAND. Good evening, Madame Séverin.

MME S. Good evening, Monsieur Fort.

FERNAND. (To GERMAINE) And try not to go to the wrong shop this time.

GERMAINE. Good evening, Monsieur. (Exit)

FERNAND. Ah, youth! ...

MME S. Aren't the evenings drawing in?

FERNAND. Mmm, mmm... autumn.

MME S. And isn't it cold? It's so cold. That child, for instance, no coat, in a flimsy little dress, almost a tutu. That's youth for you, eh. Well, what I say is - that's the way you get old before your time.

15

FERNAND. Don't talk about getting old. You don't even know what it means.

MME S. Oh no, please. You really must get it into your head that there are times when I come to see you quite simply because I want to buy something. What on earth was it, though? (Looking round) I don't know that child. Where does she come from? (Still looking round)

FERNAND. I don't know.

MME S. (Remembering) ... A litre of bleach. That's what I wanted. There's my bottle.

FERNAND. I don't sell bleach any more. Just imagine, she came to the wrong shop.

MME S. A bit dim, eh?

FERNAND. She's young. She's rather sweet. Actually, she was going to your place. Hell!

MME S. Did she say so?

FERNAND. She did say so. It went right out of my head.

(Pause)

MME S. Is that a hammock?

FERNAND. That's a hammock.

MME S. Where's Bertrand?

FERNAND. Out, at the moment. By the way, what's on at the movies?

MME S. Hamlet.

FERNAND. Still!

MME S. Oh well. So you don't sell bleach any more?

FERNAND. Bleach? No - it doesn't pay. It's a bit much, the

same film for months on end.

MME S. That'll be the day - when you do find something that pays. I keep telling you - sell your lease.

FERNAND. Oh no. No, no. Business is business.

MME S. You've no sense of responsibility. When you decide to sell something, you ought to stick to it. You're always changing. At the beginning of the year it was motor cycles. You seemed to like that, you and Bertrand. And what's the result? By March, you've given up motor cycles and gone in for ironmongery. How d'you think you're ever going to get any regular customers? Your customers never know where they are.

FERNAND. They'll get used to it.

MME S. No, they won't get used to it. And the proof of that is that next time I want to buy some bleach, and I'm your friend, what's more, well, I shall go elsewhere.

FERNAND. You'd be well advised to, because bleach - well, we've said goodbye to bleach.

MME S. It's up to you. At your age you can hardly expect advice any more. The only thing is, it'd better not stop you paying me my rent, because after all, it's my shop.

FERNAND. Yes, we know that.

MME S. And then Bertrand. You just don't realize. At his age he ought to be finding out what he wants. Well, you have a very bad influence on him.

FERNAND. Well, I haven't got a single drop of bleach left, if you really want to know.

MME S. Now I've been selling ladies' hats for nearly fifteen years.

FERNAND. Don't worry, Auntie, we won't tell anyone.

MME S. And what's happened to all your ironmongery?

17

What've you done with it?

FERNAND. And apart from the bleach, Madame Séverin, isn't there anything else you need? Some china, for instance?

MME S. China?

FERNAND. No? Ah well. Are you going to stay for dinner?

MME S. You'll drive me round the bend, you will really. Yes, a sauce-boat, Yvette's gone and broken mine.

FERNAND. A sauce-boat? Yes, we can do that for you. Shall we say Wednesday - early afternoon? Will that do?

MME S. Monsieur Fort! You're surely not going to start making china, now!

FERNAND. What d'you mean?

MME S. At your age!

FERNAND. I'm not making it...

MME S. No?

FERNAND. I'm repairing it.

MME S. Tt tt!

FERNAND. And anyway, if you really want to talk about my bad influence, Auntie, you'll have to think up something else, because this time it was Bertrand, it was his idea. Well - idea, no, he was just as it were on the ball. And that, after all, is something I have taught him - to keep his eyes open and improve the shining hour. And so, Madame Séverin, you can be proud of your little Bertrand. D'you know what he did, your Bertrand? China - quite obviously it doesn't mean a thing to you. But what he did, Bertrand, he brought me forty crates of it. Forty crates of broken china. A hell of a job, to stick it all together, of course, but you mustn't forget this: he got them for a song.

MME S. Bits of broken china, forty crates, all to be mended...

FERNAND. For a song.

MME S. For a song! And I'm sure you don't even begin to know how to mend china.

FERNAND. We're learning! Oh come on, Auntie, someone as young as you ought to appreciate that - we're learning. All you need is to be willing to learn. That's just what I was saying to that girl...

MME S. Poor child! Oh yes, though, I must go. That poor thing waiting for me, to say nothing of the cooking.

FERNAND. Careful, though - she seems a bit dim. But what's she for?

MME S. For the autumn. I mean, for the hats. You've no idea what it's like - hats, nothing but hats! But this winter I shan't be able to feel my fingers any more! So I advertised for a modiste, a young one.

FERNAND. (Thoughtful and absent-minded) Very young. Isn't life odd. She all but made a career in china. Bertrand was going to put in an advertisement. As you're coming to dinner with us, you might as well bring the girl with you..

(BERTRAND has just come in, his basin in one hand, his hat in the other)

Ah, I've slung your hammock for you. What're you doing?

BERTRAND. Good evening, Auntie. How's Yvette?

MME S. My poor Bertrand. As if I had the heart to talk about Yvette.

BERTRAND. Pity. Well, guess what. Look, boss, I'm washing my hat.

FERNAND. And about time, too!

MME S. Washing a hat! Terrible! You men are really all the same. Bertrand, come over here, I want to talk to you.

BERTRAND. In a minute. I'm busy just now. As you can see.

MME S. What's the child's name?

FERNAND. Germaine.

BERTRAND. Boss, I've got an idea.

FERNAND. We'll wait for you, Madame Séverin.

MME S. All right, all right. I'll go and get my basket.

(MADAME SÉVERIN has gone. FERNAND FORT starts laying the table. BERTRAND is washing his hat)

FERNAND. An idea, eh?

BERTRAND. Yes.

FERNAND. Is there any bread left, by the way?

BERTRAND. There's some stale bread. The baker in the rue des Trois-Moutons went broke last week. So I bought his last baking for...

FERNAND. I know, for a song. You took the bread out of his mouth, you might say.

BERTRAND. Yes. But it really is stale. You'll see.

FERNAND. The most important thing at the moment is the glue. We need a very, very great deal of glue.

BERTRAND. Have you seen the girl?

FERNAND. Yes. (A drawerful of forks somehow escapes from his hands. He picks them up) Just one of those things.

BERTRAND. Glue, glue... stick like glue... (He starts whistling under his breath)

FERNAND. It's on order. What's wrong, Bertrand – having doubts?

BERTRAND. You might have let me know, boss. Especially about the advertisement, because you said there wasn't any point.

FERNAND. (Bursting into monosyllabic laughter) Ha!

BERTRAND. Didn't you?

FERNAND. The advertisement wasn't you, and it wasn't me. The advertisement was Madame Séverin.

BERTRAND. Where is Germaine?

FERNAND. The girl?

BERTRAND. Yes.

FERNAND. Well, tell me what your idea was.

BERTRAND. Photography. Just have a look through my collection of magazines.

FERNAND. I'll put her between us, eh? The champagne glass'll be for her, don't forget.

BERTRAND. The thing is, the idea was sort of floating in the air. And then, all of a sudden, in comes Germaine. And there was the idea.

FERNAND. Photographs.

BERTRAND. Yes. You know we've got an old Kodak up there.

FERNAND. Go on, wash your hat.

BERTRAND. All we need is a couple of spots.

FERNAND. (Singing) 'Simple swallows above,
                        Fly to the one I love...'

BERTRAND. We could start tomorrow morning, if we really wanted to. We'd start with portrait photography. Real photography, that's to say. And then advertising. Get it on a proper footing... I've got some ideas for stockings. Oh, there's a lot of scope in ladies' lingerie. Sort of little tableaux vivants... And then, specialist photography, don't you think? We can launch out into nudes... Won't it get all shrivelled up, on the stove?

FERNAND. No idea. No idea.

BERTRAND. Ha! the hammock'll be a good place.

FERNAND. We'd better send a telegram to cancel the order for the glue.

BERTRAND. It'll always come in handy.

FERNAND. I've finished.

BERTRAND. So've I.

(And in fact, the table is laid and the hat is dry. They sit down)

FERNAND. Good business.

BERTRAND. What?

FERNAND. Photography.

BERTRAND. Mustn't be too optimistic.

FERNAND. Have to see.

BERTRAND. We really do need another bulb here.

FERNAND. What's more, it's almost an art.

BERTRAND. There's a bulb-holder here. (He goes over and puts a bulb in it) It is an art, boss.

FERNAND. Oh! China... china...

BERTRAND. To hell with china.

FERNAND. We'll be in trouble with Auntie.

BERTRAND. To hell with Auntie.

FERNAND. I mean on account of Germaine.

BERTRAND. (Humming) 'Simple swallows...'

FERNAND. I mean because of the spots, too.

BERTRAND. No more money, eh?

FERNAND. She's very fond of you, you know.

BERTRAND. Germaine?

FERNAND. No, not Germaine. How old d'you suppose she'd be - Madame Séverin?

BERTRAND. She's my aunt, work it out. That's a better light, eh?

FERNAND. You know, there's less and less demand for hats.

BERTRAND. Yes, yes. That's up to you, boss.

FERNAND. I rather fancy myself with a crew-cut. What do you think?

BERTRAND. No.

FERNAND. What shall I do, then?

BERTRAND. Mustn't do things you mustn't do. I'm hungry, boss, I'm hungry.

FERNAND. I'm too old. Here they are.

(Enter MADAME SÉVERIN, with a big basket, followed by GERMAINE)

BERTRAND.
FERNAND. Good evening, ladies.

23

MME S. Good evening my basket, you mean. Come in, child, they don't bite. Let me introduce Germaine.

FERNAND. We know her. Put it down there.

BERTRAND. You here and you there, me here and him there. Well, Germaine, have you found what you wanted?

FERNAND. The salt, Bertrand. I'll get the rest of the things. And the pepper, if you can. (He goes to get the bread and wine)

BERTRAND. Sit down. Why don't we put the screens up, it'll be cosier.

MME S. Help him, Germaine.

(They put up the screens)

BERTRAND. You look surprised. Don't they do such things in Pontoise?

MME S. (Sitting down) They're probably far less bored in Pontoise than they are here, my poor boy.

BERTRAND. Now we can really feel we're inside something. And here's your chair.

MME S. Well, you know, I am tired, after all. People don't realize how much energy you need to make a simple little hat.

BERTRAND. Must say it's a lousy job.

MME S. It's a job, that's all there is to it. Now what, Bertrand - changing your place?

BERTRAND. Yes, I'm going to sit at the end.

MME S. (Neutrally) He's going to sit at the end.

BERTRAND. Look at the way she's eyeing your basket; the child's dying of hunger.

24

FERNAND. (Coming back) Hands off the basket! Aperitif first!

MME S. (To the two men) So you're hungry, are you? Well, you've no right to be hungry, considering that you do nothing all day. You'll see, my dear Germaine, when you're turning out your two or three hats a day, you'll see, you probably won't be so hungry.

BERTRAND. What's in your basket, Auntie?

MME S. Nothing. A lot of heavy stuff. My arms are still killing me. 'Auntie', 'Auntie', pah!

FERNAND. Look out - I'm going to open the bottle.

MME S. Well, Mademoiselle, yes or no, do you or do you not want to work?

GERMAINE. Of course I do, Madame. I do really.

MME S. Because if you just want to amuse yourself, you'd have done better to stay in Pontoise. Hats - well, you couldn't have realized in the dark, but it's really not my fault my niece blew the fuses.

(BERTRAND brings the pepper)

BERTRAND. Of course it's not your fault, Auntie.

MME S. With eight hundred odd hats in stock you need a good constitution. And your head screwed on.

BERTRAND. Well, all those hats, you'd need a head somewhere.

FERNAND. And the champagne glass is for Mademoiselle Germaine. Aren't you going to take your coat off, Madame Séverin?

MME S. My poor Fernand! Where would I hang it?

FERNAND. Have a drink, that'll cheer you up.

MME S. There are times when one doesn't want to cheer up.

BERTRAND. Your health, Germaine.

FERNAND. Yours, Madame Séverin.

(They drink)

GERMAINE. It's bleach.

FERNAND. Yes.

BERTRAND. Yes.

MME S. Yes.

FERNAND. Never mind, I'll open another. It's just one of those things.

MME S. One of what things?

FERNAND. Come on, come on, come on... We'll pour it all back into the bottle.

(While they are pouring the bleach back into the bottle, the conversation continues)

Madame Séverin, you ought to know - how much is a spot likely to cost?

MME S. A spot, a spot - what sort of spot?

FERNAND. A spotlight.

MME S. A spotlight. A spotlight for the china?

FERNAND. How much do you think, Bertrand?

BERTRAND. Just a moment - you can't know everything just like that. Is it nice, Pontoise?

GERMAINE. No.

BERTRAND. And to think that Germaine nearly went into

the china business. And so young, too.

FERNAND. Not at all. Mademoiselle is making a career in hats.

MME S. In hats, of course! There was never any question of the china business for this poor girl; she's just lost her aunt, and she'll have quite enough trouble getting by as it is.

BERTRAND. And in there, let's have a look, eh; show us what you've got in there.

MME S. And what if I let you whistle for your dinner, one day? I wouldn't mind people bring _me_ a ready cooked meal, either.

BERTRAND. Well, here's one slice, at any rate.

FERNAND. (Coming back) The aperitif first.

BERTRAND. What about the little drop in your glass before you pour it out for the others?

FERNAND. We're all friends here. (To MADAME SÉVERIN) Don't you like our little dinners, then? Instead of eating all by yourself with your hats? All by yourself, every evening? Really!

MME S. Oh no! If you haven't any other glasses, I'm not going to drink out of these.

FERNAND. Oh hell. Are there any glasses left, Bertrand?

BERTRAND. I'll go and look. That's your slice, Germaine, that I put on your plate. You needn't wait. (He goes out)

FERNAND. He goes over there. But he knows perfectly well there aren't any glasses over there. Only, well, it's gone right out of his head. That's him all over. (He puts the bottle down and goes out the other way)

MME S. Oh, you're just too stupid, both of you. Give them to me, I'll wash them.

(She goes out with the glasses. All three exits have
been made in the time it would take to count up to
three. GERMAINE is left alone. She has the feeling
that now is the time for a key monologue, but she can't
think of anything to say. They come in again in the
same order. All three are carrying glasses)

BERTRAND. Well... Come to the wrong shop?

GERMAINE. Yes. Sort of. I don't know what got into me.
I thought... I came in...

BERTRAND. Shouldn't have gone out again...

MME S. There was a champagne glass, it's quite simple,
I never break anything as a rule, but I've broken it.

FERNAND. Doesn't matter. There was only one. Your
health.

BERTRAND. (Singing) 'In its claws, the periwinkles
Withered away and died.'

FERNAND. It's not as if it was a champagne glass that
belonged to a set of champagne glasses. Come on,
drink up.

MME S. You drink too quickly! - much too quickly. And
I'll never be able to eat all that, it's too much.

FERNAND. A slice is a slice.

BERTRAND. Have some gherkins...

MME S. A slice is a slice, yes, until one fine day your
gall-bladder bursts! Then you learn to make
distinctions.

FERNAND. (Whose knife is bending double) Who ever made
a knife like this?

BERTRAND. 'ts look.

MME S. (To GERMAINE) Haven't you ever seen a knife

28

before? Come on, eat up; don't take any notice of them. Knives! and photos, and hats, and all their childish nonsense.

FERNAND. Drink up, Germaine.

BERTRAND. Something wrong, Auntie? Is it your heart?

MME S. No. It's not my heart. Nor my liver, nor my kidneys. They're all in perfect working order. I've never felt so young. It's something else that's wrong.

BERTRAND. It's you that's wrong, eh?

FERNAND. Don't talk nonsense.

MME S. And what if I were to die, here, all of a sudden?

FERNAND. Yerss, yerss...

BERTRAND. Have a gherkin.

MME S. People do die!

FERNAND. If you were to die, Auntie, I can't imagine what would become of us, us poor bachelors.

MME S. Oh all right. Talk, talk...

BERTRAND. Have a gherkin.

MME S. I wouldn't mind some chips. If it wouldn't be depriving you.

FERNAND. 'st a minute.

BERTRAND. Have a gherkin.

FERNAND. Aren't you eating, Germaine?

BERTRAND. And a gherkin for little me.

MME S. (To the men) Because I know very well what you're getting at. I'm not such a fool, you know.

FERNAND. Bah, bah, bah. (He hums)

MME S. (To GERMAINE) But it'd be a great mistake to fall for it, my dear. You'll have security with me, and they'll have forgotten all about it long before I do.

BERTRAND. All about what?

MME S. About photography, my dear! Don't I know you.

BERTRAND. (Being conciliatory) She's terrific.

FERNAND. (Quite different) But you're the one, Madame Séverin, that says you're going to die!

BERTRAND. (Reproaching him) That's a bit much, boss...

FERNAND. Yes, well, what I say is, if you die, this poor little thing will be out in the street.

MME S. I'd like some bread.

FERNAND. And so will she.

BERTRAND. Damn, damn and damn.

FERNAND. What's the matter?

BERTRAND. I've forgotten to fix my side car.

MME S. And then I don't know Germaine very well, but I do know that it isn't everybody's cup of tea, eh, being photographed for a living.

BERTRAND. (To himself) Stupid, stupid, stupid.

FERNAND. (Trying to cut the bread) For a song. Taking the bread out of people's mouths - and how!

MME S. What do you think, Germaine? Hm, that reminds me of something that happened to me on the banks of the Marne one day. I couldn't possibly tell you, but...

BERTRAND. Mm, I must go and do it. Can't be helped.

(BERTRAND gets up)

MME S. Where are you going?

BERTRAND. I'm going to fix my side car.

FERNAND. Damn, damn, damn. Wouldn't dream of helping, would you! I just can't cut it - look!

MME S. Course you can't, seeing how stale it is.

FERNAND. Bertrand, for God's sake go and get me something that cuts! that <u>cuts</u>, do you hear me? That really cuts.

BERTRAND. Just do this and just do that! Of course! look here! really! You and your bread! And when d'you expect me to fix my side car, then? Personally, the bread!... No, but really - d'you hear him?... I don't suppose <u>you</u>'re going to offer to fix it for me, are you? My side car... the bread... no! Only, the thing is, if I don't fix it now, I never will...

FERNAND. Your side car! Good - fine - we just won't have any bread, then. All right, all right. If you only knew how little I cared!

BERTRAND. You see. (He sings a few bars of 'Simple Swallows', gets his breath back, and continues) Fernand and I, Madame Séverin, we get on pretty well, don't you think? Well, it isn't always so very funny, believe me. (He has sat down again, and goes on eating)

FERNAND. No no, Bertrand. Go and fix your old side car.

BERTRAND. Pooh, what do I care.

MME S. Well, Germaine, so you say you've got some relations on the banks of the Marne, do you?

GERMAINE. No Madame, not at all.

FERNAND. (Bitterly) Ha! not at all! - I heard her.

BERTRAND. Not properly.

FERNAND. What d'you mean, not properly?

BERTRAND. I mean - not properly! You didn't hear
properly. I was the one that was talking about the
Marne. I said I wanted to take her there in my side
car. (To GERMAINE) Didn't I? Eh? - You!

FERNAND. Wouldn't surprise me.

MME S. It's quite likely, yes. Ah, memory! All that...
It's sad, getting old like this, you know.

FERNAND. It's not much fun, no.

MME S. Especially when you haven't got anyone.

FERNAND. Especially when you haven't got anyone.

(A heavy silence)

MME S. If I had a daughter, she'd be helping me.

FERNAND. At least you've got a nephew.

MME S. Fat lot of good!

FERNAND. It's more than I've got.

BERTRAND. (Starting again) Your roast beef's always
round, isn't it, Madame Séverin?

MME S. Well, if you don't like it...

BERTRAND. Your butcher, apart from round beef, that's
all he's ever heard of, round beef.

FERNAND. There's round and round.

BERTRAND. What did you say?

FERNAND. I say there's round and round...

BERTRAND. ... the rugged rock.

(GERMAINE goes into fits of uncontrollable laughter, which she tries to stifle in her hands)

FERNAND. She's just a child; I told you.

MME S. Look who's talking.

FERNAND. And why not, Madame Séverin. I'm getting old.

MME S. Don't suppose I care, do you?

FERNAND. Because you, naturally, now that I've said I'm getting old, you've nothing to moan about any more. You don't feel the least bit old any more.

MME S. I don't? I know very well I'm old, don't talk nonsense.

FERNAND. No no, Madame Séverin - mustn't look at things like that. It's not that you're old, it's that they're young.

MME S. Have you nearly finished?

GERMAINE. (Controlling herself) Yes, Madame.

FERNAND. Well then - happy days. (He drinks)

MME S. And all that, all that just for hats! really, when you come to think of it! A whole life gone! a woman's life! you ought to have seen me when I was young! messing about with straw and flowers, ribbons and felt! And for what? For nothing! because really, really - hats! Don't you think women could do without them? because really, hats! What's the good of them? on women's heads!

BERTRAND. Gherkins?

FERNAND. That's why you have to get a move on when you're young.

MME S. Get a move on, oh la la, there's nothing I'd like better.

33

BERTRAND. Gherkin!

FERNAND. It was really Bertrand I was thinking of, when I said that...

BERTRAND. I'm a big boy now, I can speak for myself.

FERNAND. You're making a mistake, Bertrand. It's you I'm thinking of. Not me! It's not for me that I'm thinking of all the things we haven't got. And when I say that people need to get a move on when they're young, it's not me I'm thinking of.

BERTRAND. Well, it ought to be, because personally, I'm tired... I haven't the slightest desire to get a move on. If I do, it'll be some other time... Gherkin?...

MME S. (Mocking him) Tired! Tired, at his age!

FERNAND. Well, why not? It's not his fault, poor boy, if he hasn't got what it takes.

BERTRAND. (Tolerantly) What d'you mean, I haven't got what it takes?

FERNAND. No... you haven't got what it takes to make your way in the world... When you haven't got parents behind you, with money in the bank, it takes time to get going, and time, Madame Séverin, time is what makes you old! And when you think that elsewhere there are old people who have got money in the bank, and don't know what to do with it, and worry themselves sick over it, and won't lift a finger!

MME S. Who d'you mean - who won't lift a finger?

FERNAND. Not a finger, they won't lift. (He pours himself a drink)

MME S. I'm thirsty.

FERNAND. Not a finger. (He pours her out a drink)

MME S. (Suddenly on her dignity, having been thinking about

34

what is going on) Bertrand!... listen, Germaine, there's something I need to say, because we must know where we are. Oh!

(The table collapses)

BERTRAND. Well, we know where the table is at any rate.

FERNAND. Ha! Ja see that?... Ha! (He laughs loud and long)

BERTRAND. (To GERMAINE) Had you finished?

GERMAINE. Almost... I've still got a mouthful.

BERTRAND. Fernand! I'm not joking! What's this all about?

FERNAND. Aren't you funny! What's it about, what's it about... it isn't about anything. The table collapsed - that's all.

BERTRAND. Why?... Why did it collapse?

FERNAND. Just one of those things.

BERTRAND. One of what things? It oughtn't to have collapsed. I'd tied it up with a piece of rope. Where's the rope?

FERNAND. There was a rope, so there was. Good thing you told me. There was a rope, but there was also a hammock. And the hammock is the reason why there isn't a rope any more, seeing that I had to use the rope to sling it, your hammock.

BERTRAND. What about this, then? (The piece of string he was winding up at the beginning of the play is on the table. He picks it up) Isn't this a rope? I specially wound it up.

FERNAND. I don't call that rope, I call that string. That would have broken straightaway.

BERTRAND. Why did you have to interfere with my hammock, anyway?

35

FERNAND. Why didn't you interfere with it yourself, then!

(A pause. They stop it, and turn away from each other)

GERMAINE. Oh!...

BERTRAND.
FERNAND. What?

GERMAINE. Look. She... what's the matter with her?

FERNAND. Looks like a heart attack.

BERTRAND. Yep.

FERNAND. Just one of those things.

GERMAINE. That'd be just my luck. When I've just lost mine, too.

BERTRAND. Yours... your what?

GERMAINE. My Auntie, at Pontoise.

FERNAND. Hi! Auntie!

BERTRAND. (In a low voice, but with some animation)
And in any case, the hammock, you know, I'd only put it there in case I needed it. But I shan't need it, seeing that Mademoiselle, since Mademoiselle's going into the millinery business, so she won't be sleeping here, I presume.

FERNAND. Oh, really, you weren't going to make Germaine sleep in a hammock, I hope.

BERTRAND. Don't be daft. I should have slept in the hammock. And you needn't worry, Mademoiselle, there'd have been clean sheets on my bed.

GERMAINE. I don't know whether I ought to...

BERTRAND. That's the way I am.

FERNAND. What'll we do?

BERTRAND. Haven't you got some medicine?

FERNAND. Some medicine?

BERTRAND. For heart attacks.

FERNAND. No.

GERMAINE. Maybe we could go for a doctor?

FERNAND. Yes - maybe.

BERTRAND. Yes, we should... (To GERMAINE) What
    shall we do?

MME S. I wonder how much it would cost, to get a shower
    put into my place.

BERTRAND. There!

FERNAND. Depends what sort you want.

BERTRAND. That's her all over!

MME S. Cheaper than a bath, don't you think?

FERNAND. Yerss - sure to be.

BERTRAND. (To GERMAINE, who is hiding her face in her
    hands) You aren't going to cry about that, are you?

MME S. Because I really do need one.

FERNAND. Come and help me, Bertrand; then we'll be
    able to finish our dinner.

BERTRAND. All right, all right.

    (they stand the table up again)

MME S. Hm - I know what you ought to go in for, you two,
    instead of dithering all the time: sanitary appliances.

FERNAND. Not a bad idea. What d'you think, Bertrand?

(GERMAINE is still holding her head in her hands)

BERTRAND. Yes, sure.

FERNAND. We'd call it: 'Everything for hygiene.'

BERTRAND. Everything for hygiene!

MME S. And I promise you - this time I'll subsidize you. I'll sell my hats.

FERNAND. (To himself) Not at all a bad idea. The shower in all its aspects. To start with, the shower proper. And then the public shower. The communal shower. Bound to be scope for publicity there. Sort of little tableaux vivants. The compressed air shower. There's something beautiful about a shower. What do you think?

BERTRAND. We could make cars, too.

FERNAND. (Explaining his aggression) Oh, you bore me, you bore me. What's the matter with you?

BERTRAND. Dunno: I feel sad.

FERNAND. Come on, let's eat.

BERTRAND. Eat? Oh no! We've finished! What's all this about, anyway?

FERNAND. What's all what about?

BERTRAND. First it's bleach, then it's china, then it's photography, and even before it's really photography... But what becomes of me in all this?

GERMAINE. Well yes - and me?

BERTRAND. Yes, Germaine - what becomes of Germaine? Go on, both of you - eat your bananas.

FERNAND. Right. Personally, what I say is... (He stands

38

up. He's tragic) It's a question of temperament. But so far as I'm concerned, I'm quite sure I'd enjoy having a shower now and then.

MME S. No no! We won't say any more about it. Listen to me, though, Germaine. Hygiene may well be silly, but one thing you _must_ get into your head...

BERTRAND. Where are you going?

FERNAND. I heard a noise behind the screen.

(GERMAINE screams)

BERTRAND. Don't make such a row, you.

MME S. What is it?

FERNAND. There might be someone there.

BERTRAND. Come in!

FERNAND. If you shout: 'Come in', there's really no point in my putting myself out.

BERTRAND. Don't put yourself out, then. Come in, Monsieur.

MME S. How d'you know it's a man?

BERTRAND. Well, I'm not going to say: Come in, Madame, because I don't know whether it's a lady.

FERNAND. Come in... Monsieur or Madame!

MME S. Hygiene...

BERTRAND. Oh hell - come in, will you!

FERNAND. I'll go. (He disappears behind the screens)

MME S. But the thing I wanted to tell you, Germaine...

BERTRAND. Quiet a moment - I want to listen.

GERMAINE. What's going on?

BERTRAND. Pah!... Hey, Fernand, aren't you going to eat your banana?

(FERNAND comes back)

MME S. Well?

FERNAND. Well what?

MME S. I mean - what was it?

FERNAND. Ah, behind the screen? Wasn't anything.

BERTRAND. Don't you want it, Fernand?

FERNAND. You must be crazy.

BERTRAND. Just don't leave it lying about, then.

MME S. And yet I thought I heard something, too: something going: crack!

BERTRAND. (Already sarcastic) Why don't we fold it up?

MME S. What?

BERTRAND. The screen.

FERNAND. Fat lot of good that'd do.

BERTRAND. We'd get a bit of peace.

MME S. Well now - listen to me, Germaine...

BERTRAND. (Folding up the screen) Oh dear me! There certainly are moments... you make me tired, the two of you.

GERMAINE. Would you like me to help? (She stands up)

MME S. Germaine! Sit down! (She hammers on the table, which collapses all over again) What do I care! Let it

stay there. When I've got something to say, I like people
to listen to me! Now then! (Silence. BERTRAND hums:
'Simple Swallows') Bertrand!

FERNAND. Don't be cross, Madame Séverin.

MME S. You grubby little brat - just because my finger still
hurts where I pricked it with the needle on my machine,
me that made you your first pair of long trousers, you
needn't think you're going to stop me saying what I have
to say, because personally, hats! - I'm fed to the teeth
with them! Fed to the teeth, d'you hear? And especially
when you seem to think the whole outfit's just to keep
me amused, and I have a whale of a time with my hats!
As if hats amused anyone!... Lot of idiots! (She weeps)

BERTRAND. Oh all right, all right.

FERNAND. Listen, Auntie, this is all very fine, but what's
it all about?

MME S. I'm not talking to you! Now listen to me, Germaine.
My hats - it's either yes or no! And there's one thing
you must get into your head - if you don't want anything
to do with my hats, it's not only the hats that are going
to slip through your fingers! It's my capital! And when
I say capital, I mean capital! Because, after what
Yvette did to me, well, my will, you know who my
capital goes to, Bertrand? You've no idea, have you?
You poor innocent! And it isn't something to be reckoned
up in centimes, either, my capital! There's quite a
respectable number of noughts after an 8. An 8, yes!
Well, you don't know who it'll all go to, do you Germaine,
if you start making such a song and dance about everything?
Do you?

FERNAND. I don't believe it.

BERTRAND. Eh? I don't understand.

MME S. Well, answer me, Germaine.

GERMAINE. But Madame, how should I know, I've only just
come from Pontoise, I went to the wrong shop... Anyway,

if you're going to start shouting like that, no, no and no!
I'm off!

MME S. Just to think of it! That ridiculous little good-for-
nothing, that little brat with his pants hanging down!
Because I knew you, because I wiped your snotty little
nose, and what's more, when you had the chicken-pox, yes,
the chicken-pox and all your rotten little brat's diseases...

BERTRDAND. Am I asking you for anything? Is anyone here
asking anything from anyone? What's all this deluge of
idiotic words? Chicken-pox - well - I've had it, and you
don't get it a second time, who wants to talk about
chicken-pox any more? Auntie! If you really want to
make up to me for all the chicken-poxes I had when I
was a kid, Auntie, by giving me your 8 or 80 or 800,000
or 8 million francs, well and good, Auntie, give them
to me! If it gives you any pleasure to give them to me.
But really, there's no reason to get so excited about it,
because I'm not asking you for anything.

FERNAND. You're making a mistake, Bertrand.

MME S. Well, if you're not asking me for anything, you
won't get anything, you young layabout!

FERNAND. Oh, but he should.

MME S. Not a penny!

FERNAND. Auntie! Just enough to buy a couple of spots!

MME S. What?

FERNAND. (To BERTRAND, to put him on his guard) You
just keep quiet.

BERTRAND. Oh, the spots - they're for now! Not for when
she's dead! When you're dead, Auntie, I don't know
what'll be happening to me, I might be dead myself, and
you know where you can put your 8 million then!

MME S. Guttersnipe!

BERTRAND. Your will, your hats, what do I want with them?
They're for Mademoiselle - Mademoiselle, I make you
a present of them. And as far as anything else goes, I'm
not asking anyone for anything. And as for making a song
and dance about things, it's not Germaine who needs
preaching at, Auntie! You don't have to look any farther
than yourself.

MME S. Say something to him - or I'm off.

FERNAND. Bertrand - help me up with the table, will you.

BERTRAND. (Coldly) That's enough. Shut up. Anyway, I'm
going to fix my side car. It couldn't be simpler: I'm
going to fix my side car.

(He's just about to go out, but he's let go of the screen.
It sways, and falls over on MADAME SÉVERIN's head)

GERMAINE. Oh!

FERNAND. Bertrand! Oh, that had to happen, that just had
to happen!

BERTRAND. People shouldn't annoy me, that's all.

GERMAINE. Oh dear, oh dear...

(She looks as if she's going to faint. Possibly because
part of the screen fell on her too. FERNAND stood it
up, and it immediately fell over again)

BERTRAND. You don't really know me, Germaine. I'm not
usually like this.

(He fusses over her a good deal more than is really
necessary)

FERNAND. He's not usually like that, Auntie, you mustn't
be cross with him.

BERTRAND. You'll see - tomorrow I'll take you to the
Marne in my side car; how would you like that?

FERNAND. Come on, Auntie, don't sulk.

GERMAINE. I don't know: it isn't Sunday.

BERTRAND. I'll take your photo.

FERNAND. Bertrand!

BERTRAND. I'm not usually like this.

FERNAND. Bertrand, for God's sake! (Aside) The
hammock! What a good idea the hammock was! (He
carries MADAME SÉVERIN over to the hammock)
Bertrand!

BERTRAND. That's right, the hammock... Come on,
Germaine, come and have a rest in the hammock...

GERMAINE. No...

FERNAND. (They are both carrying a woman in their arms)
You skunk! You rotten little skunk!

BERTRAND. Eh? What? Eh?

FERNAND. Not usually like this, eh? Oh no, and how you're
not, not usually like this. Oh no!

BERTRAND. What is it, Fernand? Eh? What's the matter?

FERNAND. Nothing. Everything's terrific. You can put her
down on the ground. (He makes MADAME SÉVERIN
comfortable in the hammock)

BERTRAND. Germaine! What's wrong? What d'you want me
to do?

FERNAND. Put her down on the ground! She hasn't done
you any harm - that's all you ever think about. Leave
the girl alone.

BERTRAND. No no, it's not that - we're just going to sit
down. (He sits down, with GERMAINE on his knees)

44

FERNAND. Doesn't the shop look wonderful, hm? What does it remind you of?

BERTRAND. We'll get used to it, Fernand... don't get so excited.

FERNAND. What?

BERTRAND. I mean to say: we'll tidy it up, we'll tidy the shop up.

FERNAND. One day I shall just go away.

BERTRAND. Where, Fernand?

FERNAND. Away: I shall just go away.

BERTRAND. Where?

FERNAND. Away. What d'you expect me to do here?

BERTRAND. What do I expect you to do here, eh, you lazy bastard? And what about the photography, huh?

FERNAND. And what about the film, you non-existent bastard?

BERTRAND. Let me talk to Germaine.

FERNAND. What are we going to buy the film with? I haven't even got anything to sit on any more.

GERMAINE. (Getting up) Do sit down, Monsieur.

FERNAND. I don't even want to sit down any more.

BERTRAND. How did I ever come to get mixed up with such a nit!

FERNAND. One day you'll be sorry for talking to me like this.

BERTRAND. Well, aren't I right, Germaine?

FERNAND. In the meantime I'm going to look for some vinegar. I'm going to make a big effort to find the vinegar bottle. Yes, the vinegar. (He goes out)

BERTRAND. Fernand! Oh look here, Fernand... Oh dear oh dear oh dear oh dear oh dear!... What a life. I just don't know any more - I just simply do - not - know.

GERMAINE. Paris really is a peculiar place.

BERTRAND. What? Oh no, it's the same everywhere. You get tired, tired...

GERMAINE. You ought to go to bed.

BERTRAND. Oh yes! We'll go to bed, won't we. And who's going to wake up tomorrow morning? We are, as usual. We're going to wake up. (Calling) Fernand! No, the thing is, it's that... the thing is, do you know what it is, Mademoiselle? The things is, that we don't know what we want. We don't know what we want.

GERMAINE. Yes.

BERTRAND. What d'you mean - yes? Isn't it true, what I've just said? Look - no need to go any further - you! You, for instance: what do you want? Eh?

GERMAINE. I don't know.

BERTRAND. Well - have you ever been photographed before?

GERMAINE. A bit.

BERTRAND. Yes. A bit. But it's not your profession. You've just been photographed like everyone else. Only, when it comes to being photographed seriously, no one's interested any more. So long as it doesn't give them any trouble, everyone's dead keen, of course they are. Far more of them than you need. Just like with love. May I, Mademoiselle? Oh but of course, Monsieur, please do. When it comes to waving their legs in the air, there's no shortage, everything's sweetness and light. The only thing is, that afterwards, when it's a question of looking

after the brats, and the chicken-poxes, and the housework, and the washing up, hm! It's not the same thing
at all, that's not what I was looking for, if only I'd
known, yammer yammer bla bla - and no one's interested!
Well, I've had enough! If you want to be properly
photographed, you can go elsewhere, my dear! This is
it, I'm shutting up shop, no more bits of fluff for me.
Get out of it!
And don't cry like that! But Good God, what've I done?
Oh look, I didn't ask for anything, did I? Here I am,
I'm always rushing around making myself useful, I
can't have a minute to myself to do nothing in, just look
at that bulb, who told me to fix it, eh? No one. Well
then. That doesn't make me cry.
... Oh come on now, stop crying. No, of course not,
things aren't always so very funny. I know they're not.
Even when you have character, even when you're
ambitious. It's not enough just to be ambitious in a
vague sort of way. You have to know what you want.
Oh dear me! If only I knew what I wanted! ... You think
you want something... and then you discover you don't.
Do you think I want to go in for photography? Photography! photography... well, I'm just not interested
in photography, and that's it.

GERMAINE. It's not true - you do care about photography.

BERTRAND. I do?

GERMAINE. It's not true - you do care about photography.
You say that - you only say that to make me cry.

BERTRAND. Think so?

GERMAINE. If I said that I'd like to go in for photography
with you, you wouldn't say that...

BERTRAND. You?

GERMAINE. But I would like to! I'd like to do photography
with you.

BERTRAND. It's not true.

47

GERMAINE. Yes it is! It is! Well then!

BERTRAND. Now I don't know where I am! Why do you want to do photography with me?

GERMAINE. I don't know. I've no idea.

BERTRAND. (Worried) Aha!

GERMAINE. And the housework, too, and the washing up, too!...

BERTRAND. Mustn't get so carried away, Germaine.

GERMAINE. Oh, you know, when I start crying, I never know what I might do.

BERTRAND. In the first place, we haven't any film.

GERMAINE. We'll buy some.

BERTRAND. We haven't any money.

GERMAINE. We'll ask Auntie.

BERTRAND. And what if Auntie doesn't want to?

GERMAINE. Doesn't matter if Auntie doesn't want to. All that matters is that we want to!

BERTRAND. Oh, Germaine!

GERMAINE. Oh, Bertrand! - what did I say? Oh! what did I say!

BERTRAND. Mm - I've no idea - what did you say?

GERMAINE. I called you Bertrand!

BERTRAND. That's the first time anyone called Germaine has called me Bertrand.

GERMAINE. (Considering the situation) Oh, what a mess! (She runs out in some confusion)

(Enter FERNAND)

FERNAND. Here's the vinegar! Well! Even so, good evening!
God, I'm fed up! I must look charming with my glass of
vinegar. Hey, Madame Séverin! (To the shop) You see!
What d'you expect me to do?

BERTRAND. You know, boss... that poor girl's in a bad way.

FERNAND. Hm, it's in a fine state, my shop.

BERTRAND. You know what she wants to do?

FERNAND. No.

BERTRAND. Look, there's no point in standing there with
your vinegar. Pour some over her head.

FERNAND. Ah yes...

BERTRAND. She wants to do photography.

FERNAND. Really?

BERTRAND. Yes. Well, my dear fellow... D'you call that
a knot?

FERNAND. I never could make knots that stayed put.

BERTRAND. Unwise. Can you imagine Germaine in a photo?

FERNAND. It would probably be better if you tied them
again.

BERTRAND. It's not her line. (He tightens one of the knots)
Photography, I mean: Germaine.

FERNAND. Is vinegar supposed to be drunk or rubbed in?

BERTRAND. Rubbed in, I think. She'd start with portraits,
and then full-lengths, and then nudes. Personally, I
don't think it's her line.

FERNAND. Here, don't tie it too tight. If she falls out, it'll

49

probably make Auntie laugh. I know her. When you come to think of it, your characters are pretty much the same.

BERTRAND. You know who she thought of, to photograph her?

FERNAND. Yes.

BERTRAND. Yes.

FERNAND. Well then - ask Auntie for some money for some film.

BERTRAND. She won't. She's too tough.

FERNAND. (Sings) 'Simple Swallows'.

BERTRAND. Go on, give her the vinegar.

MME S. I don't need your old vinegar.

FERNAND. It's here, though. Mustn't waste it.

MME S. I don't want it.

FERNAND. All right, all right.

BERTRAND. Feeling better?

MME S. Yes. I'm going.

FERNAND. Shall I help you?

MME S. No, no; I'm all right.

BERTRAND. Good, fine; well, I'm going to bed.

MME S. Bertrand!

BERTRAND. (Coming back: he had been going to find GERMAINE) Yes, Auntie?

MME S. Bertrand - there's something I really would like to

tell you, all the same. And you too, Fernand.

(FERNAND is singing, absent-mindedly)

Fernand!

FERNAND. Yes, yes. What is it?

MME S. Listen, both of you. I don't know what you think of that child, Germaine.

FERNAND.
BERTRAND. Er.... .

MME S. But in any case, there's one thing I do know. Which is that I, Raymonde Séverin, or Auntie, or whatever you like to call me, well, there's one thing I would like to tell you...

(The hammock gives. MADAME SÉVERIN falls, and crumples up)

BERTRAND. The knot!

FERNAND. Plonk! Only to be expected.

BERTRAND. It's my fault, I suppose?

FERNAND. It's certainly not mine!

BERTRAND. You're not really going to say it's my fault?

FERNAND. No, it's not your fault.

BERTRAND. Whose fault is it, then?

FERNAND. It isn't anyone's fault. It's just one of those things.

BERTRAND. Well, er, yes.

FERNAND. Is something wrong? Where does it hurt now?

BERTRAND. Hey, Auntie.

FERNAND. Is it here? Is it there?

MME S. You and your hammock!

FERNAND. Ah well, what can you expect, Auntie, it's just one of those things. Hm! you'll certainly have to forget about your hats for a day or so. Would you like a little vinegar?

MME S. You and your hammock!

FERNAND. Well, yes, just one of those things. Come on, Bertrand, do something.

BERTRAND. Why, is she really hurt?

FERNAND. I've no idea, but I heard something go: crack.

BERTRAND. (At the street door, through which GERMAINE fled) Germaine! Hey! Germaine!

ACT TWO

(The same shop; it is now full of hats and clocks. GERMAINE is making a hat. MADAME SÉVERIN is crossing the stage, leaning on two sticks, but having less difficulty than she'd like to make out. GERMAINE has just got up to help her. They are whispering, as if they were at someone's deathbed)

MME S. Don't get up!

GERMAINE. I want to!

MME S. No!

GERMAINE. Don't get up!

MME S. I want to.

GERMAINE. It'll tire you.

MME S. Oh, be quiet. (In a normal tone of voice) Yes, but look here! What's the time?

GERMAINE. Shh!

MME S. (Fairly quietly) At this hour!

GERMAINE. (Very quietly) I'll bring them over to you.

MME S. (Fairly quietly) Sit down or I'll scream.

GERMAINE. (Very quietly) Shh!

(MADAME SÉVERIN bangs on the floor with one of her sticks)

GERMAINE. (Fairly quietly) Shh!

MME S. (Fairly quietly) Damn!

GERMAINE. (Very quietly) Shh! What with your sticks...

MME S. (Moderately) My sticks, my sticks. You have to lean on something in this world.

GERMAINE. (Also moderately, but more forcefully and less passionately) Yes, but your sticks, if you don't want anyone to help you, why don't you leave them in the umbrella stand? You'll be able to walk quicker, and they won't get mixed up with your feet and trip you up.

MME S. My sticks.

GERMAINE. They're over there, your croissants.

MME S. My croissants.

GERMAINE. (Retiring into her shell) Good evening, then.

MME S. Yes but yes but - but don't get the idea that you're wrong. I can do without your help, thank you very much. You just stay in your corner. I'll go and get my croissants myself! I can see them perfectly well, over there, by themselves, all three of them, in my corner. And I'm going over to it because it is my corner. The corner they keep for me. For me. Nothing to do with you. Excuse me, Mademoiselle, you can get on with your work. (She starts off tentatively)

FERNAND. (Behind the screens, lets out a yell)

GERMAINE. You win.

MME S. What's the time?

GERMAINE. (Very quietly) No, he's gone back to sleep.

MME S. (Very quietly) He's having a nightmare.

GERMAINE. (Very quietly) Shh!

MME S. (Walks over to her croissants... stops)
Germaine...

GERMAINE. (On her feet) Are you all right?

MME S. Sit down!... Just let me see you put a bit of guts
into what you're doing. Guts, yes. Oh!... I'm not
saying you should work faster! - go to it, like
lightning, just look at her, can't see her needle now,
she's so quick! - No! - guts, I said, and I don't
call that guts, what you're doing.

GERMAINE. (Very quietly) Shh!

MME S. (Fairly quietly) No. That's not it. That's not guts.

GERMAINE. I shan't say another word.

MME S. I'm not asking you for anything. Yes, there is
something a bit odd about my slipper. But that's my
problem... Don't stop working. If you have the slightest
idea what work is. It's when I walk. I lift my foot up,
I don't feel a thing, it's quite all right. I put it down
again, gently, very gently... click! and that's it. Did
you hear it?

GERMAINE. No.

MME S. Well, now it's as if my big toe was in a draught.

GERMAINE. A hole?

MME S. No. I've looked. It's like a sort of trickle of air
between the sole and the... Like under a door, when
it's cold... (Symbolically) Like winter!

GERMAINE. Oh no.

MME S. Oh yes. Come and help me. I feel quite weak.

GERMAINE. (Dropping some of her material) Bugger!

MME S. (Starting to walk again, in despair. Feebly) Youth!

GERMAINE. (loudly) What?

(Another yell from FERNAND)

MME S. Those men! Why don't they go somewhere else, why don't they go away! - with their clocks! - and their stupidity! - and their china! What?

GERMAINE. Nothing.

MME S. And you can go away too, with them, and with your hats!

GERMAINE. My hats?

MME S. Mine!

GERMAINE. Yes, but do think...

(A pause)

MME S. (More softly) ... that you don't even know how to make. What on earth's this? Is it coffee or is it chocolate?

GERMAINE. It's a mixture of the two.

MME S. So you mix things... In my day, we chose.

(Sound of hammering next door)

GERMAINE. They're at it again.

MME S. My shop! What are they doing to my poor shop?

GERMAINE. You'll see - it'll be all right, judging by the way they've begun. Modern, and everything.

MME S. Yes; only it isn't mine any more. Ah well, they can make a lavatory out of it, for all I care.

GERMAINE. Oh!

MME S. I mean it. And I sold it for them! For my legs, to
mend my poor legs, after what they did to them with
their hammock. Marvellous, their hammock. The whole
neighbourhood's still splitting its sides over it. But
this is my home, now. Which is just too bad for them.
They can get out!

GERMAINE. Careful! You don't want to fall over, do you?
Get out! ... Of course they'd get out, if they knew where
to go. And anyway, you know what their latest idea is,
don't you? - to go into business.

MME S. Business! and where is their famous business?
China, photographs, clocks? That's a new one, that is,
clocks.

GERMAINE. They're feeling their way.

MME S. They're always feeling their way... and they never
find it!

GERMAINE. But Madame Séverin - we're young!

MME S. What of it?

GERMAINE. Well - it's just that when you're young, you
have to be patient.

MME S. Nonsense, of course you don't need to be patient
when you're young! What sort of an idea is that, hm?

GERMAINE. I don't know.

MME S. You never know anything. Listen, Arlette,
Thingummy, Camille, tcha! - what's your name again?

GERMAINE. Germaine.

MME S. We'll throw them out, and that'll be the end of
them. You don't know how to make a hat, but you could
learn. That's something that people can learn. When
they're young. Instead of being patient. I've just got to

teach you a few wrinkles, and we're off, it'll be like a snowball. Hats, well, they're hats, there's always a steady demand. What's got into my croissants today, they're terribly stale. And anyway, I shall die soon, you might think that one over. That ought to cheer you up.

GERMAINE. There's another one finished. Isn't it lovely?

MME S. Well? I rather think I said something, didn't I?

GERMAINE. Auntie! Don't talk so loudly!

MME S. Well, answer me then! And then I won't talk so loudly. Is it yes or is it no?

GERMAINE. Me? I can't tell you - I don't know.

MME S. Even so, you have to choose: hats with me, or the door with them.

GERMAINE. You mean me?

MME S. Yes, you.

GERMAINE. Oh goodness!

MME S. All right; leave me alone, now. I'm eating. - She doesn't know. - She doesn't know a thing, ever. When you're young, you don't know anything. Hurry up and get old, for goodness' sake. You're like... a bit of croissant, it's as simple as that. It doesn't know much, either, a bit of croissant... then, hey presto, it lets itself get eaten up, and that's the end of it. A stale bit, though, a bit of stale croissant - well, it's already beginning to know what it wants; it doesn't let itself be eaten up as easily as you do. Take it as a model - get stale.

(FERNAND, who has up to now been invisible behind the screen, lets out a yell, wakes up, and gets up. He's in pyjamas)

FERNAND. Aïe aïe aïe! Oh la la! Oh, I'm fed up with it.

It's the same every night. Ah, you're there, are you?
It's pitch dark, and I have a nightmare. I wake up in the
middle of the night and then I can't get to sleep again.
That sort of thing gets you down in the end, you know,
Françoise, oh, Monique, Mauricette, Thingummy...

GERMAINE. Germaine.

FERNAND. Ah yes, Germaine. Well, my night's finished.
I shan't get any more sleep now. What's the time?

GERMAINE. Between eleven and twelve, Monsieur Fort.

FERNAND. What? You should have woken me before. Makes
me look such a fool. Where's Bertrand?

GERMAINE. He's out.

FERNAND. Out. What time did you say it was? (He consults
a few clocks) 11.20? 11.10? 11.30? 11.30! What about
it, then? What about it?

GERMAINE. What's the matter?

FERNAND. The table! Just look at it! Why isn't it laid?

GERMAINE. I'll lay it now.

FERNAND. I should think so, too! What next, eh. At half
past eleven - no, at twenty to twelve! Congratulations!
That's really something. I wonder how it'd be if you'd
had a night like I have: three in the morning, and I still
hadn't slept a wink, on that rotten old pile of hats! Once
upon a time I had a bed - now I've got a pile of hats.

GERMAINE. Bertrand offered you his hammock.

FERNAND. Of course he did. The hammock. And in the
meantime, his lordship has gone out. Where to, eh?
Pah! - as if I cared. All right, fine, let him go out.
Only, the next time you see him you might tell him to
take all his clocks with him. There are too many clocks
here. You can't even find out what time it is any more.
And anyway, I don't like clocks - I don't! - and I've told

him so. He needn't count on me if he's going into the
clock trade. They give me the willies, clocks do.
Tick tock, tick tock, tick, tock, just listen to them,
what a stupid noise! And what's more, this is my place!
This is my place, my dear, and what I think about clocks!
... I don't know what I think, but in any case, you just
don't feel you're at home any more. (He's just about to
sit on the newly-finished hat)

GERMAINE. My hat!

FERNAND. And there's no point in arguing about it, either.
There are too many hats in this house, as well. Far too
many. And that's my last word. (He sits down and studies
the hat) What d'you expect anyone to say about a thing
like that? You don't know where you are any more.

GERMAINE. I'll put it away in its box.

FERNAND. (Catching sight of MADAME SÉVERIN) Ah! So
there she is! (To GERMAINE) There she is! (To
MADAME SÉVERIN) So you're there, are you?... But
what what what - what's she up to in her little corner?
Eh? (To GERMAINE) Good Lord! She's eating croissants!
(To MADAME SÉVERIN) Very nice, eh? (To GERMAINE)
Funny, isn't she? (To MADAME SÉVERIN) Well,
Auntie, did you sleep well? Was it nice, Fernand's nice
big bed, the nice big beddy-byes with its great big
mattress? Eh? She wouldn't have a teensy bit of
croissant to spare, would she, for her hungry little
Fernand?

MME S. Leave my croissants alone, you low-life!

FERNAND. (To GERMAINE) Low-life! (To MADAME
SÉVERIN) So you're feeling better than you were
yesterday, then?

MME S. None of your business.

FERNAND. Mm, well, if I were you, Auntie, I reckon I'd
be a bit worried. Your doctor strikes me as being a
funny sort of joker. Just guess what he told me last
night. He said: my dear fellow, your Auntie won't live

through the night. Eh? What d'you think of that? It's
irresponsible. When someone tells you you won't live
through the night, well, you just don't live through the
night, and that's that. Or else that someone doesn't
call himself a doctor. Don't you think? Isn't that so?
When you think of all the people you can't trust. Eh?
Well, what d'you think? Frankly?

MME S. Yes...

FERNAND. What! Then you don't think so?

MME S. Tell me...

FERNAND. It's just like my breakfast - they tell me all this,
that and the other. And the net result: who has to go
without his breakfast?

MME S. Monsieur Fort...

FERNAND. Yes - Monsieur Fort does.

MME S. You know, Monsieur Fort, if you wanted to be very
kind, you'd go and buy me a bottle of aspirin.

FERNAND. Of course. A bottle of aspirin. Right away.

GERMAINE. Wait a moment, Monsieur Fort - I'll heat you
up a cup of chocolate.

FERNAND. I wouldn't think of it.

GERMAINE. With some bread and jam...

FERNAND. Wouldn't think of it...

GERMAINE. Because I haven't got any butter left.

FERNAND. No no no; it's very kind of you both. I'll have a
coffee at the café over the road.

GERMAINE. Oh no, Monsieur Fort! Not in pyjamas!

FERNAND. I ought to be dressed at this hour! Listen to me,

Denise, Miriam, what's-your-name, Marie-Antoinette...

GERMAINE. Germaine.

FERNAND. If you like. We mustn't forget that we got you here to mend china! Bertrand and I, we were sitting pretty, we'd just bought forty crates of broken bits. Now, since you've been here, who's been dealing with the china? Eh? You have, maybe? Or Bertrand? Or Auntie, perhaps? There's only one person who's stuck to it, the famous china, and that's me, always me, me again, and now, as the final insult, I'm supposed to hide myself! However, if I put on my raincoat, perhaps you'll be so good as not to raise any objections.

(He does so, and in doing so, he continues)

As for Monsieur Bertrand, if he isn't interested in china any longer, it may well not be his fault. But, strong as I am, everyone has his weaknesses, and you mustn't be too surprised if I sometimes get discouraged, too. 58 pieces! That's quite something, 58 pieces. Well, yesterday, I made a vase out of 58 pieces. A big vase. As big as that. Some pieces, to get them right, I had to use a nail file. Yes. (A harsh little laugh) Well, when I'd finished it, so it'd dry more quickly, you follow me? I put it out in the air. Not a bad idea, eh? Well, it fell out of the window. Plonk! If you'd like to pick up the pieces, they're still on the pavement. And I can guarantee there are more than 58.

(While speaking, he has been feeling in his pockets)

GERMAINE. Are you looking for something?

FERNAND. Yes. There's no point, though. You couldn't do me a small favour, could you, Germaine?

GERMAINE. Oh yes - of course I could.

FERNAND. That's nice of you. Because it would be a bore to have to change a 5,000 franc note just to buy a bottle of aspirin. I haven't got a scrap of change. So if you could lend me a couple of hundred francs, say, I could get my packet of Gauloises as well as the aspirins.

GERMAINE. Oh, but the thing is, I haven't any money left at all, Monsieur Fort.

FERNAND. Oh.

GERMAINE. You can give me your 5,000 francs, if you like, and I'll pop out and change them, there's a post office not far away.

FERNAND. Yes, but where do you expect me to get 5,000 francs? Eh? It's not the least bit important, though. Some people still throw their fag-ends away in the street. You only have to bend down and pick them up.

GERMAINE. Oh no!

FERNAND. Well, dear, just say I was lying, and let's forget about it. (He sits down)

GERMAINE. Bertrand's sure to be back soon, it's twelve o'clock.

FERNAND. Yes, of course; and after all, the aspirin isn't so urgent.

(FERNAND and GERMAINE look at MADAME SÉVERIN)

MME S. (Sings) 'Simple swallows...'

FERNAND. You know, Auntie... There's the goodwill of my business.

(MADAME SÉVERIN stops singing)

My goodwill, yes! What's the matter? I can sell it. Who to?

MME S. (Doesn't understand) Who to?

FERNAND. Who to. Aye, there's the rub. To be or not to be. Let's just assume - may I, Auntie?... (He goes over to her) - let's assume, my goodwill, that I sell

it to my friend Duchenard. He's a good lad, is old
Duchenard. Now what he's interested in is the launder-
ette business. Let's assume he arrives here with his
machines. I say to him: Good, fine, it's a deal, I'll
let you off paying for my goodwill, I don't want any
money, your machines are enough for me, you make
me sub-manager of your laundry, you pay my rent to
old Ma Séverin, and we'll be snug as a couple of bugs.
This is all hypothetical, Auntie, because Duchenard,
he'd be only too willing, he's a good lad, old Duchenard
is, I only have to put up my 'to be let' notice, and he'll
be there. Well, you know the first thing Duchenard
would do? (To GERMAINE) You know what Duchenard
would do?

GERMAINE. Duchenard? I don't know him.

FERNAND. (To MADAME SÉVERIN) Well, Duchenard
would start by throwing you out. Oh yes, Auntie. He'd
say: Auntie, go and eat your croissants in Timbuctoo.

GERMAINE. Oh!

FERNAND. Mm! - I shouldn't like that at all, because I'm
very fond of you, Auntie. And I'm sure you wouldn't
like it either, seeing that your nephew Bertrand, by the
same token, after all, they certainly need clocks in
Timbuctoo, he would deem it a pleasure, he'd go with
you. If that's what you really want.

MME S. No; what I really want, if you don't mind, is for you
to put the screens all round me. There are some screens
over there. Because, before lunch, I'd really like a
moment or two of solitude. At my age, you need solitude.
It's quite true. So if you'd like to put those screens up
all round me, that would suit me. That's all.

FERNAND. That's all.

MME S. And after that, I'll give you some money to go and
get me some aspirin.

FERNAND. Yes. No - but you know what I mean, don't you?
I'll go and get your screens. (He does) You see, Auntie,

we have our difficulties, Bertrand and I. You'd be the first to suffer, you being so helpless, you see what I mean? Having to rely on other people's good will when you want some screens fetched, eh? Your travelling days are over. Well, if I had to sell the lease of my shop, I don't say to Duchenard, I say to somebody, and even to you, Auntie, well, what then? You'd be the first to suffer. No but after all, Auntie, I'm not your nephew. I don't ask anybody to take an interest in me. Only, the way I am, Auntie, I just can't help myself, I'm very fond of your nephew. He's so shy. He doesn't dare ask you himself. I tell you, though, and I've got nothing to gain, but I tell you: if you've got some money, take advantage of it before you're dead. Yes, take advantage of it. Give Bertrand a bit, he's a good boy; if I know him he'll take good care of you and brighten up your last days.

(He has put the screens up, except on the side facing the audience)

MME S. Well, you know, there are times when you just don't want anyone to talk to you. Quite frankly, it irritates me to hear your voice coming into my ears. So if you wouldn't mind shutting the front door, if you can, eh? So I can have a bit of peace until lunch time.

(A short pause)

Yes, all right, I'm going to give you a little money for the aspirin. Here, take it. You can keep the change.

FERNAND. Oh, there's no reason to...

MME S. Yes there is - here, here's a hundred francs.

(She pushes the note through the last little gap in the screens, and then closes it completely)

See you later.

FERNAND. (Folds the hundred-franc note in four, in eight, in sixteen, in thirty-two and in sixty-four, then puts it in his pocket. After which he sings) 'Simple swallows'.

GERMAINE. You know, Monsieur Fort, I think I probably
could mend some of the china... You'll just have to
show me what to do...

(But FERNAND goes on singing. He's looking for a
notice)

If Bertrand had told me what to do with all these clocks
I'd have got down to them long ago. But I don't know.
They're going. They aren't all going the same, but I
suppose that's quite normal, for clocks.

(FERNAND discovers the notice: Lease for sale, all
trades)

Oh! I can't believe it... Oh God oh God, what on earth
shall I do? Wait a moment, Monsieur Fort. At least
wait till lunch time.

FERNAND. This is the end, the end, the end.

(FERNAND is just going to put his notice up when
BERTRAND enters, carrying an enormous sack)

BERTRAND. Are you crazy? Give that to me!

FERNAND. No, I will not give it to you! I won't give you
my notice! You're not a real friend! Bertrand! I just
can't stand it any more! I want to live! I'm still young!
You can take your clocks back! Take anything you like -
I've given you all I've got! but leave me my notice!
Leave me my notice, Bertrand, please! You're
stronger than I am; if you tug like that you'll tear it!
My notice! Will you let go of it! Let go of it!

BERTRAND. All right, all right. Keep your old notice -
do anything you like with it. Oh la la... people are so...
How's, um...

GERMAINE. Germaine.

BERTRAND. I know. Here you are, here are the little
pigeons for lunch, and a tin of French beans. The
little pigeons are going to be steak today.

FERNAND. Give me a cigarette.

BERTRAND. Here you are. That's a fine thing. You can't turn your back for a single moment... Well, anyhow, thanks! The clocks are still here! No one's touched them, eh? No one's likely to touch them. I really begin to wonder why I take the trouble to bring you any clocks.

GERMAINE. Oh, I'm so sorry, Bertrand, but you didn't tell me what to do with them so I didn't know.

BERTRAND. You couldn't have shown a bit of initiative, I suppose? The two of you. I say to you: here are some clocks! You just have to do the best you can with them, I don't know any more about them than you do. Even so, even so - you don't have to be a magician to do something with a clock. What's your brain for?

FERNAND. (Pointing to Bertrand's sack) And that, what is it this time?

BERTRAND. Oh, nothing. Where's Auntie?

FERNAND. You can answer me first, can't you?... What's that?

BERTRAND. I'm not asking you what's in there, I'm asking you where Auntie is.

FERNAND. Eh? What have you thought up now? Eh? So you don't want to say!

BERTRAND. Pipe down. Where's Auntie?

FERNAND. Auntie isn't here! Auntie's gone out! Out! Look! (He points to the screens) There, there, there - she's gone out! Poor little fellow with his great big sack! Let's have a look... No, damn it, let's have a look!

BERTRAND. (To GERMAINE) Go on, go and start cooking all this stuff.

FERNAND. He's not going to tell you. What if it's horse

shit, eh? After the clocks there'd be nothing so extraordinary in that. He's not fussy. So long as he's working,
it's all the same to him if it's horse shit. It doesn't
occur to him that maybe horse shit isn't selling very
well this year, good Lord no! So long as he's working,
he's happy. Eh? Isn't that so? Ah, so it isn't horse
shit, then? Were you afraid Mademoiselle might be
sick of it all - of the horse shit, the little bits of china,
and all God's dear little creatures?

BERTRAND. Fernand, Fernand, Fernand, Fernand...
what's the matter, old man, you're so pale, you're
in your pyjamas - what's the matter? Haven't you had
any breakfast this morning?

GERMAINE. No, he hasn't had any breakfast.

BERTRAND. Here. I owe you this. Quick, go and have
your coffee.

FERNAND. Thanks, thanks. You're really not such a bad
chap. Be nice to him, Antoinette, Thingummy, Simone,
Mademoiselle. He's a good photographer, really,
Bertrand is, you know. (He's just going out, but he
can't keep back a phrase that he suddenly finds is in
his head. He turns and shouts it out as he goes through
the door) Yes, but, I, I, I... Well, I'm not a
photographer! You see! (He goes out)

GERMAINE. Good morning.

BERTRAND. I've already said good morning.

GERMAINE. Can I see what it is?

BERTRAND. No no, it's nothing. It's nothing to do with
business. It's just for fun. Oh, and anyway... I don't
know why I bothered with it. I think I'll just quite
simply go and throw it in the dustbin. I don't know what
got into me.

GERMAINE. The dustbin's too small.

BERTRAND. We'll make little parcels every day.

GERMAINE. All right.

BERTRAND. Oh la la... there's nothing extraordinary about it, you know. It isn't horse shit. Mustn't think I mind saying what it is.

GERMAINE. But there isn't any point, seeing that we're going to throw it away.

BERTRAND. Well, you aren't curious.

GERMAINE. No.

BERTRAND. It's nuts.

GERMAINE. Nuts?

BERTRAND. Yes - nuts!

GERMAINE. To eat?

BERTRAND. No, to crack. I thought we might amuse ourselves cracking nuts.

GERMAINE. That's a good idea... yes, we might amuse ourselves...

BERTRAND. Yes. And then there's another thing, you can sell them, shelled nuts. There are some confectioners, for instance, who need them.

GERMAINE. Yes.

BERTRAND. Yes...

(They say nothing for a moment, the situation being so awkward, but then)

GERMAINE. It's nice, not to say anything for a while, isn't it, Bertrand?

BERTRAND. It's not that I'm not saying anything... I was listening to something in the street.

GERMAINE. Something?

BERTRAND. Yes, something.

GERMAINE. I didn't hear anything.

BERTRAND. No... you don't have to hear things. Some people hear one thing, others another. It all depends.

GERMAINE. You ought to have told me.

BERTRAND. Told you? There's nothing extraordinary about it, you know. I just happened to be listening. It wasn't worth listening to on purpose.

GERMAINE. What was it?

BERTRAND. No, and then, if I'd felt like saying something to you, it would certainly have been something else. And then it would have distracted me, and I wouldn't have heard anything at all. You see. People say: if only I'd known this, or that; but that isn't the way it is. If I'd known, it wouldn't have been the same at all.

GERMAINE. But now that you <u>have</u> heard it, there's no reason why you shouldn't tell me what it was.

BERTRAND. It was a little whistle; with two holes, you know, a tin whistle, with a sort of angle to it... a kind of flat whistle, the angle's about a third of the way down, like that... I don't remember which end you blow through, though. I never had a whistle like that. I think you blow down the narrow end. Eh? don't you?

GERMAINE. I don't remember.

BERTRAND. Some kid must have been amusing himself blowing it.

GERMAINE. Yes.

BERTRAND. You didn't hear it, then?

GERMAINE. No.

70

BERTRAND. Funny. I didn't dream it, though... No, you see, here we are, in the same room, we're not doing anything, we both have ears, and yet one of us hears something and the other doesn't.

GERMAINE. Er... yes...

BERTRAND. Perhaps you heard something else. That I didn't hear.

GERMAINE. No, I wasn't listening.

BERTRAND. Everyone can't be listening at the same time. Maybe, while I was listening, you were looking, so you'll have seen something I didn't see. Did you?

GERMAINE. No. I didn't see anything special.

BERTRAND. Well, you must have been doing something. People are always doing something.

GERMAINE. No, I wasn't. I was waiting.

(BERTRAND gives up)

BERTRAND. Aren't you cold?

GERMAINE. No.

BERTRAND. I am.

GERMAINE. We can put another log on.

BERTRAND. Then you'll be too hot.

GERMAINE. (After a silence) Bertrand!...

BERTRAND. Yes, my name's Bertrand. And yours... yours is Germaine.

GERMAINE. Don't you like it?

BERTRAND. Yes. But it just goes to show that we're not the same:

GERMAINE. Not the same?... No, of course we're not the same. And it's just as well! Because, well, if you were called Germaine, I wouldn't like it.

BERTRAND. And you do like me being called Bertrand?

GERMAINE. Um... yes, I do, rather.

BERTRAND. What a funny girl you are. It just doesn't mean a thing to me, being called Bertrand. I can't imagine how anyone can like it. Hm? how come?

GERMAINE. You mean... I don't know, I can't explain...

BERTRAND. What's the use of talking, then? Huh! You're there, I'm not saying a word, I'm just minding my own business, and listening to a little toy whistle, not asking anything from anybody, and then Mademoiselle decides that that won't do, someone's got to say something... Right, fine, I'm all for it, let's talk! Only, when it comes to really saying something, when it comes to communicating - nothing doing! Why make such a hullabaloo about it, then? If that's the way it is, all you have to do is just keep quiet.

GERMAINE. But Bertrand! - I'm not asking you for anything! Nothing at all. Oh my goodness no, I've got other things to do, you know.

BERTRAND. Oh what a bore! Oh mother! what a bore! Listen to me, my girl: not only am I supposed to say something, but what's bloody more, I'm not allowed to say anything! No-thing what-so-e-ver! because it irritates the little lady! - Well, you just be irritated! I'm going to put another log on. I won't say another word.

GERMAINE. It's not my fault if I'm quick-tempered. I know very well I am. Even so, though, you mustn't talk to me like that. I've always been told I've got sensitive nerves.

BERTRAND. Oh! It's not that your nerves are sensitive. It's that you get on mine.

GERMAINE. Well, I'll go then: so what.

BERTRAND. Germaine!

GERMAINE. I tell you: so what, so what, so what.

BERTRAND. No one's allowed to go when someone's just put a log on the stove for their especial benefit.

GERMAINE. Not true!

BERTRAND. Not allowed!

GERMAINE. Well, I just don't care... Oh dear...

BERTRAND. Soppy... soppy little... soppy little milkmaid!

GERMAINE. Well, what d'you expect? I came to the wrong shop, all right, but that's not so difficult to understand... The number, it was dark, you couldn't see... All I was thinking about was making hats, I wasn't expecting miracles, well, put yourself in my place... And then, there it is, I'm here, I don't say a word, I don't make trouble, they said they wanted to do some photography, fine!... and all this and that, what d'you expect me to think. And where d'you suppose I could have slept, that night? If that's how it was, when I wasn't asking for anything, oh my poor Auntie... well, you shouldn't have said that. There. You just try and say that's not how it was.

BERTRAND. Well, you know, it's true, what you say. Mm - true.

GERMAINE. It is. Isn't it?

BERTRAND. It's true. I'm sure it's true.

GERMAINE. Me too; I was sure it was true.

BERTRAND. Only... only, only only!... Only, if that was the only thing that was true in the whole business, it'd be too good to be true. There's something else that's as true as that, and even a bit truer. You see?

GERMAINE. Really?

BERTRAND. Yes.

GERMAINE. What is it?

BERTRAND. I've no idea.

GERMAINE. Oh...

BERTRAND. When I say that I've no idea... What I do know
is that I've got a sort of heavy feeling in my stomach.
At this moment... but I don't know what it is.

GERMAINE. A stomach-ache?

BERTRAND. Yes. There, at the moment... because it isn't
always there that I get this heavy feeling. If it wasn't for
that, well, of course! you'd tell me that I'd just eaten
a salami sandwich. But a salami sandwich - I know what
that's like. Even when I have trouble with my digestion -
I don't mean a sandwich, I mean something like
sauerkraut and frankfurters, for instance, and God
knows how difficult that is to digest! Well, I don't
think it's worth talking about. So if I do talk about it,
it must mean it's something else.

GERMAINE. That wasn't nice of you, Bertrand - you ought
to have told me. Then I wouldn't have bored you with
my troubles.

BERTRAND. You say it's not so difficult to understand you,
though. Pff! well, naturally, of course I understand you!
You came to the wrong shop, it was dark, you'd just been
to your Aunt's funeral. And so on. I understand, you see!
Only, tell me: is that all you want - for me to understand
you? ha ha ha ha ha ha! - careful! I'm asking you a
difficult question. Is that all you want - for me to
understand you? Because if that's all you want, you can
go, you've got what you wanted - I've understood you
for a long time, it's all over, you've had it, bye-bye,
look after yourself. Hm? What d'you think? Think before
you answer.

GERMAINE. I'm glad you understand me...

BERTRAND. You're glad. Good. Fine. So'm I. And then what?

GERMAINE. How d'you mean?

BERTRAND. Well? It's just what I was saying: you're staying put.

GERMAINE. Of course I am! You don't go away just when you've found someóne who understands you.

BERTRAND. Quite. You stay put. But that's not all you want - for me to understand you. I've got to do something else to you, now. What have I got to do to you?

GERMAINE. To me?

BERTRAND. Yes, to you! Since you're here.

GERMAINE. I don't know. I've no idea...

BERTRAND. Well - neither have I! I've no idea! I don't know what it is, but it's here! Here! because it isn't the salami sandwich that's weighing on my stomach! I could have eaten eight salami sandwiches like that one! That's not what's stopping me breathing! and you have the nerve to say you're not asking me for anything!

GERMAINE. But since I don't know what it is...!

BERTRAND. Exactly! There's nothing worse! Who does know what it is, then, if you don't, and if I don't? No one knows, yes? no? or does someone know? Who is it, then, who is it?

GERMAINE. Listen, Bertrand, you know perfectly well that it was dark... you know perfectly well that no one could have seen the number, and that if I came to the wrong shop...

BERTRAND. Oh no, for goodness' sake, for goodness' sake... Really, for goodness' sake, you must stop telling me about that all the time.

GERMAINE. I'd love to tell you about something else, but what? Bertrand...

BERTRAND. I'm tired, tired, tired. A bright young man like me - and I used to be so full of energy - spending all my time changing light bulbs, messing about with side cars... yes, that's what I've turned into... And in no time, too. Look at me, go on, just look at me! with my arms dangling - I'm as flabby as a cowpat! At least I hope you remember, the evening you arrived, do you remember I pinched your bottom?

GERMAINE. Oh Bertrand! I know you didn't do it on purpose!

BERTRAND. Yes, but I did. That's how I was. Of a practical disposition. Direct. No shilly-shallying. Not everyone likes that sort of thing, of course - doesn't always come off, but on the whole you see the world, you aren't often idle. And in the mornings, a glutton for work! The sun! black coffee, shoes not polished. That's how I was. And I liked them to be called Solange, when they were called Solange, and some were called Solange. But you! When I started to pinch your bottom, you simply didn't believe it!

GERMAINE. Oh, but I did!

BERTRAND. Oh no you didn't! And there's another thing, I knew one called Ursula! Yes, Ursula! Well, when I called her Ursula it was like getting hold of a hammer by the handle! I'd say: Ursula! and it was as if I'd already got my hands on her. But you, you! when I call you Germaine, you know what it does to me? I'm ashamed.

GERMAINE. You mustn't be...

BERTRAND. No? Really not? Well then, Germaine, tell me how this little thing unbuttons?

GERMAINE. Bertrand!

BERTRAND. I ask you because I'd like to see what's inside, Germaine... may I?... may I?... may I, yes or no?

GERMAINE. No!

BERTRAND. You see. That's not what you want from me.

GERMAINE. Not like that, Bertrand.

BERTRAND. Bertrand!... Yes. When you call me Bertrand now, I'm sunk, you've got me. Carry on, then - what d'you want to do with me? Because, after all, you're not going to be content to stop there, are you? I'm quite sure you're not going to be content with giving me stomach cramps. You'll have to make up your mind. What _do_ you want?

GERMAINE. I don't know...

BERTRAND. You never know anything!... What do you want?

GERMAINE. I... I'd like to do some photography with you.

BERTRAND. Not true.

GERMAINE. It is, really is it. I _would_ like to.

BERTRAND. Not true. You're there, aren't you? I can see you, can't I? You're visible, no? I don't need a Kodak to see you with. And anyway, I've had enough of girls who need to be photographed before you can see them. Why not the cinema, while you're about it?

GERMAINE. But Bertrand, you were the one who wanted us to go in for photography together.

BERTRAND. Right. Undress, then. I wanted to take nudes. Well? are you going to undress, hm? Want me to help you?

GERMAINE. No!... What must I take off?

BERTRAND. Everything.

GERMAINE. Right. Er... you go and get your camera.

BERTRAND. Oh no, I'm not in any hurry. Go on, go on. And anyway, I need to know whether it's worth the trouble.

GERMAINE. Bertrand!... Bertrand, why are you so unkind? You're unkind.

BERTRAND. I tell you, Germaine, if this goes on, I... I don't know what I'll do, I just don't know, and I don't want to know, either, but... but I'll do it!

GERMAINE. Oh! Why are you so unkind?

BERTRAND. Go away! Go away! No, not that way: take the pigeons! and the French beans! go on! make yourself useful! it's not so difficult to make yourself useful! So make yourself useful!

GERMAINE. I haven't got any butter...

BERTRAND. Here's some! Bit of luck it hasn't melted! Get going! and see we get something to eat! Do you hear me? Something to eat!

(She's gone. BERTRAND, thoughtfully, starts cracking the nuts)

To be or not to be. Well, that's not the question. I'm quite willing, personally. What's a nut? Nothing, nothing at all. A nut is a nut. Cracking a nut is cracking a nut. On the one hand you crack nuts, and on the other hand you mend broken china. And maybe if someone were to come tomorrow and ask me to mend the nuts I've cracked today, I might not say no. Otherwise, otherwise, otherwise, they shouldn't have invented nut-crackers, the bastards. Personally I take things as I find them! It's fun, cracking nuts. When I was a little boy the noise made me laugh. Crack.
Only now, though, you have to be careful not to damage the insides, because they take themselves seriously in the confectionery business. The inside's like a little brain, so gently does it! No one has any right, eh?

No one has any right to damage your little brains. Got to be careful. Got to be polite. Polite, eh!... Alas, poor Yorick!... Well, I'm going to crack them how I like, they're my nuts. Because, after all, there's one thing that mustn't be forgotten, and that is that to buy them, to buy my nuts, I had to sell my side-car... my side-car! Why did I have to sell my side-car...?

(He drops everything and weeps)

The bastards... the bastards... What have they done with my youth?

ACT THREE

(The hats have taken over the shop. You know where
you are. It's only the screens, now, that give the
impression of hiding anything. The clocks are still there,
but they're stowed away in the hammock, waiting to
be packed. There is also a motor-cycle wheel somewhere, and a dressmaker's dummy, with a white dress
on it that makes it look like Germaine. The table is
laid for tea for four, because it is five o'clock on a
Sunday afternoon. MADAME SÉVERIN and FERNAND
are vaguely smartened up for Sunday, like the table.
FERNAND is photographing MADAME SÉVERIN's head
with an old Kodak on a stand. They both have ladies'
hats on their heads)

FERNAND. (Fiddling with the Kodak) Oh, come on. Even
   so, you really must, to believe it! ...

MME S. To believe it... What?

FERNAND. What she says.

MME S. But that's just it - she hasn't said anything.

FERNAND. But that is just it - if she hasn't said anything,
   eh! If she hasn't said anything! ... Then it's easy.

MME S. Yes. Because she didn't have anything to say.

FERNAND. Oh no, not at all, Not at all. Hm, if that's what
   you think! Well, just because someone doesn't say
   anything, if you think it's because he hasn't got anything

to say! My poor friend! - I knew a Chinese girl, once!
No taller than that! And just a child - butter wouldn't
melt in her mouth. Well, perhaps it would, but you could
have spanked her bottom, she looked so like a little girl
who wouldn't have known what it meant.

MME S. And what happened?

FERNAND. What happened? A Chinese girl, I tell you, what's
more. Well, believe it or not...

MME S. Believe what?

FERNAND. Well, what do you expect me to say: she never
stopped talking.

MME S. Oh, look here, Fernand... really!...

FERNAND. Eh? what? now what've I said? Well, there was
this Chinese girl, say what you like, she never stopped
talking, but...

MME S. But what?

FERNAND. But she hadn't got anything to say. Only, to
show you that it isn't because...

MME S. Oh, really!

FERNAND. But it's just the opposite! For example, take
someone who has got something to say, well, usually
he doesn't say a word. That sort of person. He doesn't
say a word.

MME S. Why not?

FERNAND. It just happens like that.

MME S. Oh no!

FERNAND. What d'you mean: oh no!

MME S. Oh no. When you have something to say, you say it.

FERNAND. Oh well of course, if you look at it like that, but as I said, usually...

MME S. Usually...

FERNAND. Usually, when you have something to say...

MME S. You say it.

FERNAND. Not always! It depends what it is.

MME S. Oh come on, do get a move on.

FERNAND. I'm allowed to clean my lens, aren't I?

MME S. After all this time.

FERNAND. And anyway, what on earth are you talking about? That wasn't what I said!

MME S. Don't say anything, then.

FERNAND. All right, I won't say anything. And what does that prove?

MME S. It proves that you haven't got anything to say to me.

FERNAND. Not at all! And the proof of that is that I've got something to say to you at this very moment, I'm even dying to say it, but I'm not saying it.

MME S. What is it?

FERNAND. Er... no - I'm just not going to say it.

MME S. Oh look here... Oh really, Fernand! What _are_ you getting at?

FERNAND. I'm trying to show you that if Germaine didn't tell you anything, it's only because she decided to keep it to herself.

MME S. Well, that's a fine thing. No manners.

FERNAND. On the contrary; it's just when you have got good manners that you keep things to yourself.

MME S. Well, I'd have preferred her to say it right out. Instead of keeping it to herself like that.

FERNAND. I say she kept it to herself... Germaine probably didn't really want to. It's just that she didn't dare, that's all.

MME S. Didn't dare what?

FERNAND. Tell you.

MME S. Tell me what?

FERNAND. How should I know? If she didn't tell you, why should she have told me?

MME S. Then we just don't know.

FERNAND. No. We just don't know.

(A pause)

MME S. And anyway, I can't see why she should have told me that.

FERNAND. Don't move.

MME S. I'm not moving.

FERNAND. Excuse me! There, you've just moved again.

MME S. I'm not moving now. Hurry up.

(A pause)

FERNAND. Don't move.

MME S. I'm not moving.

FERNAND. You aren't moving - only you really are moving, because you're thinking of something else.

MME S. My tart's in the oven.

FERNAND. What of it? So it's in the oven. Your tart - it's better off there than anywhere else.

MME S. Are you ready?

FERNAND. Mm hm. Go on, then!

MME S. What d'you mean: go on? Go on... ?

FERNAND. Smile!

MME S. Ah!

FERNAND. Good! Fine! Don't move now... Your hat.

MME S. What about my hat?

FERNAND. You haven't changed your hat.

MME S. Are you sure?

FERNAND. Look, Auntie, I know it's Sunday...

MME S. It could be. (She takes her hat off) Hurry up, then.

FERNAND. 'Hurry' ...

MME S. What?

FERNAND. No, but look here, Auntie!...

MME S. Oh yes! Well, give it to me, then!

FERNAND. Eh? Oh!

(They change hats)

MME S. In any case, if there is something she wants to tell me, I bet you anything you like she'll say it. And any minute now, what's more.

FERNAND. Well, if I were you, I'd ask her. Just sort of

casually. Nothing in my hands, nothing in my pockets...

MME S. Yes of course... Do you mind getting back to your Kodak?

FERNAND. Well, what I say...

MME S. Ready?

FERNAND. Marvellous. Pity it isn't in colour.

MME S. Get a move on, then; take me.

FERNAND. Right, let's go, I'll take you. But don't move.

MME S. I'm not moving, now.

FERNAND. Your photo, eh?

MME S. How do you mean, my photo?

FERNAND. That's what you want me to take, isn't it? No - because you said: take me, so I need to know what you mean.

MME S. Oh really, Fernand, this isn't the moment.

FERNAND. Right, then smile. There! Hold it! There's a little birdie, a tiny little birdie, that's... coming... out...

MME S. This is the last.

FERNAND. This is the last... a little birdie coming out... Tch tch. It's not a little birdie in there. But it is something. And something that's moving. What on earth can it be?

MME S. Oh, really; listen, I...

FERNAND. Don't move, don't move; I can see what it is.

MME S. Don't move, don't move! You aren't thinking about my tart.

FERNAND. You told me it was in the oven.

MME S. That's just it.

FERNAND. Well then you don't need to bother about it - it's cooking!

MME S. Oh, I know these tarts, they don't cook for long. When they think they've been cooking long enough, they start to burn.

FERNAND. What sort of tart is it, your tart?

MME S. A cheese tart.

(FERNAND pricks up his ears)

What is it?

FERNAND. That's them, isn't it?

MME S. Who?

FERNAND. On the motor bike.

MME S. Oh no.

FERNAND. No, it's not them. Just a moment! It'll only take me a second. I've only got to unscrew the lens. When I've unscrewed it I'll just have to screw it up again and I'll be with you. There's a fly in it.

MME S. A fly? There aren't any flies in January.

FERNAND. It must be a fly left over from last summer that's woken up. Just one of those things. A fly wakes up - and then it needs a bit of time to warm itself up.

MME S. All right... kill it... and then let's...

FERNAND. Of course! Of course I'll kill it, I mean. Look, here it is... you'll see, when you're as old as it is... (He blows on it)

MME S. Me?

FERNAND. What of it? (He blows) You see, it isn't even
strong enough to fly away.

MME S. I'm not worried: I'll never be like that.

FERNAND. People don't realize.

MME S. In the first place, it may be a fly from next summer
that's a bit early. Go on, screw away.

FERNAND. Eh?

MME S. Your lens.

FERNAND. (Who is following the fly step by step) There's
no hurry, they aren't back yet.

MME S. Screw it in, all the same.

FERNAND. And anyway, I've already taken you.

MME S. Taken me? How d'you mean: taken me?

FERNAND. Really, old girl, that's all you ever think about!
Eh? What's the matter? Is it the spring, or what?

(The fly has led him over to MADAME SÉVERIN. He
takes advantage of the opportunity to paw her a bit)

MME S. Well, have you taken me?

FERNAND. Yes, I didn't tell you, but I've already squeezed
the whatsit.

MME S. You might have told me.

FERNAND. Don't move. I want to squeeze it again...

MME S. When Bertrand comes.

FERNAND. ... just to make sure.

MME S. Ah!

FERNAND. What?

MME S. The fly's climbing all over me...

FERNAND. Poor old thing.

MME S. And anyway, why isn't he back?

FERNAND. Bertrand?

MME S. Yes, Bertrand; I can't imagine what he can be doing.

FERNAND. Pah! Have you ever seen Bertrand do anything?

MME S. What about you, then, what do _you_ do? What _are_ you doing?

FERNAND. Nothing, like Bertrand. I'm looking for the fly. Oh dear, it's in a hurry - look. Simple souls, these little creatures.

MME S. Not at all!

FERNAND. Like swallows, eh? 'Simple swallows...'

MME S. Oh really! Bertrand!

FERNAND. Not Bertrand - Fernand. Not my fault if Bertrand isn't here. _I'm_ here, and Bertrand's somewhere else. You might say that that's the big difference between Bertrand and me at the moment, don't you think?

MME S. Yes, well, come on, then, Fernand, that's quite enough.

FERNAND. Apart from that, I'm quite willing to change names. Since I'm the one that's here. It's as if I were to call you Germaine, isn't it? - isn't it, Germaine dear... Isn't it? Well then, Germaine! Come on...

(They knock the Kodak over. FERNAND lets go of Auntie; it gave him a shock)

MME S. Hey!

FERNAND. 'tsall right, nothing's happened, my Kodak fell over.

MME S. Well yes... It's better that way.

(They listen in silence)

FERNAND. I thought I heard them.

MME S. No, that's not them. Good, well then... (She's just about to go out, but stops to put her hat on the dummy's head) Doesn't white suit her, hm?

FERNAND. (Furious) They ought to be back! At this hour, people are back! for tea. Here, give me that. (He picks up the Kodak and goes and puts it away)

MME S. How long does a tart take to cook, in your opinion?

FERNAND. In the oven?

MME S. Yes.

FERNAND. It depends on the oven.

MME S. I must go and look, then. (She goes out)

FERNAND. And then, it depends on what cheese you put in the tart. (Bitterly) It depends on what cheese you put in the tart! What cheese. The tart. The cheese tart. Oh, what a nit. Tralala, la, la, lalalalala la. (He sits down and reads an old magazine) Hm! Well I never! In the Bay of Biscay! Hey Auntie.

MME S. What?

FERNAND. The obelisk; you know?

MME S. What obelisk?

FERNAND. Last week's obelisk, you know. (He turns over the page) The one the English were towing... (he reads) in a steel cylinder! 'The obelisk had been put in a steel cylinder equipped with a rudder, bla bla bla... and was being towed by a little steamer called the <u>Olga</u>'.

MME S. Cleopatra's needle?

FERNAND. Yes. Well, it got shipwrecked in the Bay of Biscay.

MME S. Oh yes, I remember.

FERNAND. In the Bay of Biscay. In French waters, that's to say. Oh hell. (He reads) 'We have described how Cleopatra's needle was found off Ferrol by the steam-ship <u>Fitz-Maurice.</u> '

(MADAME SÉVERIN comes back)

Here, look at this. There's a beautiful engraving: 'The shipwreck of Cleopatra's needle. '

MME S. Mm hm, I remember.

FERNAND. What d'you mean, you remember! We haven't got up to that bit, yet.

MME S. I've had the thing long enough, you don't suppose I haven't had time to read it, do you? I knew it by heart when I was eight years old. Just think, its was my grandmother's father, on my father's side, that is, who gave them to me when he died.

FERNAND. Huh, that's a good one! (He reads) 'The captain...' - just listen to this: 'The captain is refusing to give up the obelisk unless the English government pays him a large sum of money. '

MME S. Yes, but he was an Englishman. It's in London, Cleopatra's needle. They've stuck it up, since then. It's the English Place de la Concorde.

FERNAND. Really?

MME S. Just look it up, it's in the number dated November 1877.

FERNAND. Yerss, yerss... (he reads)

MME S. It smells good, doesn't it?

FERNAND. What does?

MME S. My cheese tart.

FERNAND. Yerss.

MME S. It's cooking; very, very gently.

FERNAND. Yes, gently. That's life!

MME S. A Chinese girl. What was all that you were saying about a Chinese girl?

FERNAND. Who, me?

MME S. Yes, you. As if you'd known a Chinese girl.

FERNAND. I did. That's right.

MME S. Where? When?

FERNAND. When I was doing my military service.

MME S. Ah, I see! Ah, because you did your military service there?

FERNAND. (Still reading) There, yes, in...

MME S. In Saigon?

FERNAND. Goodness no, in... in a town that's much better known than that...

MME S. Oh, go on! As famous as all that?

FERNAND. Oh, how stupid, I can't remember the name of it... Limoges! I did my military service in Limoges!

MME S. Do they have Chinese girls in Limoges?

FERNAND. No, there was only one.

MME S. What was she doing there?

(FERNAND makes a gesture implying that he doesn't know)

Which only goes to show that it's quite true that the yellow races are insinuating themselves everywhere. It's as if I were to go and insinuate myself into Shanghai, in the barracks.

FERNAND. (Still absorbed in his reading) I say, the war in the East isn't going all that well.

(The sudden sound of an electric machine brings the conversation to a halt. It is coming from the next door shop. The noise stops)

I'd love to know who's going to win. The Russians or the Turks.

MME S. The Russians.

FERNAND. Oh good, I'm so glad. The Turks look rather gruesome.

(The noise again)

I can't help wondering how you got hold of her; you certainly seem to have picked a winner.

MME S. I didn't ask her what she did. I just had to sell my shop: that was all there was to it.

FERNAND. Because you couldn't have dreamed up a better neighbour, however hard you'd tried. Even on Sundays. You tell yourself, it's Sunday, we won't have the machine today - but not at all. Even on Sundays, we have the machine.

MME S. But my dear Fernand, look here, if you'd wanted me to keep my little shop, next door to the big one, hm? - you ought to have been a bit more careful. It was terribly nice of you to make me so comfortable in the hammock, but all the same, in the circumstances, all the same! It's your own fault for not checking the knots.

FERNAND. To say nothing of the fact that she must be so bored, poor little thing, working away all by herself on a Sunday afternoon.

MME S. Because, if you remember, it's not so very long that I've been able to walk without my sticks.

FERNAND. The Circassians - are they Russians or Turks?

MME S. Oh, the Circassians...

FERNAND. It's like the Bashi-bazouks, I never know where I am with them.

MME S. The Bashi-bazouks...

(A pause)

FERNAND. There's a hell of a smell of cheese, don't you think?

MME S. Oh... the cheese...

FERNAND. Yes, oh!... All that stuff... (He throws the magazine down. Noticing the dummy with the hat on) Oh, really, after all. Eh?

MME S. What?

FERNAND. The hat... it's not so bad as all that. When you see it like that, with a dress underneath, one that really goes with it. It's certainly got... well, style, eh? (He runs his hands over the dummy) Don't you think? That there's something er, um, hm about it? I mean to say...

MME S. All right! it's a hat! it's quite nice, but that's all.

FERNAND. Well, yes, but... I just wouldn't have thought, when... (He realizes he's putting his foot in it) I'll just go and have a little look at your tart, because there really is a smell of cheese, you know.

MME S. All right, all right - leave it to me, will you? Up to now I've been the one that makes the tarts and hats in this household.

FERNAND. I'm thirsty.

MME S. You're always thirsty. (She goes out)

FERNAND. Yes, up to now I've been the one that's always thirsty in this household. (He drinks the remains of a bottle of Vermouth. Loudly, to MADAME SÉVERIN) Ah! Sundays! Gay, aren't they!

(Noise of the electric machine for a few seconds)

I'm going to have to screw my lens in again.

(He goes out into the street, humming 'Simple swallows'. He shuts the door behind him. MADAME SÉVERIN can be heard singing: 'Simple swallows'. Then one of the alarm clocks starts ringing, and goes on for a long time)

MME S. (Off) Can't you stop it? Lazy thing!

(The alarm stops of its own accord. MADAME SÉVERIN continues)

(Off) I'm beginning to get sick of all these clocks, and pendulums, and alarms. He really has got to get rid of them, the little layabout! If I leave it there, it'll burn; if I take it out, cold cheese isn't worth eating. Oh la la, what a bore! (She comes in with the tart) It's just too bad. If they don't come - we're grown-up, we can eat it on our own.

(She notices that FERNAND has gone out, puts the tart down and goes and listens near the wall on the right. FERNAND can be vaguely heard gossiping with the neighbour. After a moment MADAME SÉVERIN decides to join him. She goes out. The stage is empty. An alarm clock starts ringing and gently fades away.

The hat falls off the dummy. MADAME SÉVERIN's
voice interrupts FERNAND's chat with the neighbour.
Then silence. Then the sound of the electric machine.
FERNAND comes back, followed by MADAME SÉVERIN.
A pause. Then FERNAND yells furiously, above the
noise)

FERNAND. Now we'll have to put up with it for the rest of
the afternoon!

MME S. (Yelling) What? What?

FERNAND. (Yelling) Very clever! Oof! There are times
when I don't know what I wouldn't...

MME S. (Yelling) What was that you said? But what was it?
What did you say? Say that again!

FERNAND. (Defying her) Yah, yah, yah!

(The neighbour stops her electric machine. In the
silence)

Huh! Very clever. Much good that's done us.

MME S. What was it you said? You just say it again, eh.

FERNAND. No.

MME S. You don't want to say it again.

FERNAND. No. What for?

MME S. Because I didn't hear it.

FERNAND. So what. There are things you sometimes say
when there's a lot of noise, and then when there isn't
any more noise, well, it's not the same, so you don't
want to say them any more.

MME S. Well, bravo. Congratulations. At your age, that's
certainly the best anyone could expect!...

FERNAND. I can still smell cheese.

MME S. A little girl! A little girl who does the best she can,
with the very latest equipment, to earn her living, and
to keep her old father, who hasn't got anything left...

FERNAND. Obviously - he's dead.

MME S. (Not hearing him) ... A little girl, with hardly any
clothes on, a tutu, a confirmation dress, practically!
An innocent little angel, and his lordship - his lordship
has nothing better to do than hang round her all day:
at his age!

FERNAND. Who, me? Hang around that little, er...

MME S. You might just as well say it: that little trollop,
yes!

FERNAND. Oh, come on...

MME S. What do you mean, come on!... You don't think
I don't see her little game, do you?... We wiggle our
hips, we pull our skirt up to our thighs, oh do sit down,
Monsieur - and there we are, he's already frothing at
the mouth. But my dear Fernand, do you think I wasn't
up to all those tricks long before your time? Me too -
I had whole squadrons of men after me. All I had to do
was shrug my shoulders. There's no point in playing
the injured innocent with me, you know.

FERNAND. Oh well, so far as injured innocence goes...
Ah, there's your cheese tart.

MME S. But - aren't you going to say it isn't true?

FERNAND. Of course it's not true; really, Auntie! At my
age!

MME S. You're a hypocrite! A hypocrite! Just look at him!
He looks like a Turk!

FERNAND. A Turk, eh? Oh no, really! A Turk - that's
going a bit _too_ far!

MME S. But why should you think _I_ care, whether you hang

around the child or not! and even supposing you managed
to make her, why should you imagine it would worry <u>me</u>?

FERNAND. I've no idea.

MME S. Hm? at my age.

FERNAND. I really don't know if it would worry you or not,
but...

MME S. If she likes you, why should I see any harm in it?

FERNAND. But she doesn't like me, for God's sake!

MME S. Oh! the idea hadn't crossed your mind! Had it,
Bertrand! Eh?...

FERNAND. Certainly not. And in the first place, my name
isn't Bertrand. That's just it. And then it's not my
fault if I make the child laugh. She hasn't got that much
to amuse her. (He is still wearing the lady's hat)

MME S. What?

FERNAND. I say, if I make her laugh. I amuse her. What
d'you expect? Just now, she began to laugh the minute
she saw me come in. Well! That's a good thing, isn't
it? When she's always so sad. You just ought to have
seen her! Ha! Doubled up, she was. And I'm telling
you - she only had to look at me, I didn't even have
to try to be funny.

MME S. She laughed, did she?

FERNAND. Yes. She laughed. She even split her sides.
Without wanting to blow my own trumpet, the fact is,
she split her sides laughing. Well then...

MME S. So she split her sides laughing, did she?

FERNAND. Well, yes.

MME S. Hm; she had good reason.

(A pause)

FERNAND. What? she had good reason? What does that mean: she had good reason?

MME S. Oh yes, she had good reason.

FERNAND. What?...What is it?... Is there something special about me?

MME S. Vaguely, yes.

FERNAND. Oh, go on. What will you think up next. The child just laughed, she didn't have any ulterior motive.

MME S. Oh no, of course not. Considering what you've got on your head.

(A pause. FERNAND becomes aware of his hat)

FERNAND. Yerss. Yerss... I don't really see what's so very funny about that. You're, um... Yes, one might say you're naive! If you think that's what...

MME S. If it wasn't that, I'd very much like to know what it was.

FERNAND. Yes. Oh, let's skip it.

MME S. Go on, tell me!

FERNAND. Tell you my foot!

MME S. You and your illusions!

FERNAND. And anyway, those that have ears to hear, let them hear! and those who don't have eyes to see - well, they just won't see anything at all.

MME S. Yes, well, you can leave my tart alone.

FERNAND. It'll get cold.

MME S. That's no reason to put my hat on it.

(She picks up the tart)

FERNAND. What do you want me to do with it, then? Ah...
(He puts it on the dummy. And notices the one on the
ground) And this one's to play football with, I suppose?

MME S. (To her tart) What's the time?

FERNAND. I don't know. (He picks the hat up and puts it
on his head) With all these clocks, it takes a bit of
working out. Just a sec, eh, and I'll tell you.

(He starts adding up the time on all the clocks)

MME S. Well, I'm certainly not going to put it back in the
oven.

FERNAND. I would, if I were you. And eleven are forty-two...

MME S. And what would you be doing in the meantime,
Bertrand?

FERNAND. I'd be working it out. And eight are fifty. And
anyway, don't call me Bertrand. Bertrand here,
Bertrand there, it annoys me.

MME S. Oh la la... Oh, I'm so tired. If I could only rely
on you, Fernand.

FERNAND. Go and put your tart back in the oven, Bertrand
won't be long now.

MME S. Yes, and the moment I set foot in the kitchen he'll
be outside. Running around wagging his tail, the gaga
old fool.

FERNAND. Who's 'he'?

MME S. You know very well who I'm talking about.

FERNAND. Oh, get on with it - you and your tart. Your
gaga old fool won't budge. 58 and 4 are 62.

MME S. Because... you just want to see him when he really

gets down to it. It's all very well wagging your tail, but you just ought to see him when he's got his back to the wall.

FERNAND. Not my fault.

MME S. No, it's mine.

FERNAND. Last night? It just couldn't be helped, Auntie, last night: I tried terribly hard to think of other things, as usual, but I couldn't make it. The thing is, you see, that you have a sort of presence.

MME S. Oh yes.

FERNAND. Yes, More and more. Your volume, everything. When you're there, well, whatever I do, I just can't manage it any more. I can't act as if you're not there. A hundred and nine. All I have to do now is divide by the number of clocks. The thing is... You can't say the same about everyone, you know!

MME S. One day, I'll just go away.

FERNAND. With your tart?

(A pause. FERNAND realizes he's gone a bit too far)

No, I didn't mean it, you know.

MME S. Bertrand...

FERNAND. Fernand.

MME S. Fernand... If you really want to make that child laugh... I...

FERNAND. 'Course I don't.

MME S. Hm! Just to look at you...

FERNAND. But what on earth are they doing? Good God, what are they doing? Three eights are twenty-four, plus five, twenty-nine. Carry two: 8 ones are 8, and

2 are 10, 8 point 9 hours. Nine-tenths, that's to say,
which makes it somewhere around five to nine! On an
average, of course, because I'm talking statistically,
but... He needs this tyre, though, doesn't he? So why
doesn't he come and fetch it? No really, who do they
think they are? at five to nine?

MME S. All right, I'll go and put it back in the oven.

(FERNAND is aware of the disillusionment in MADAME
SÉVERIN's voice)

FERNAND. Auntie...

MME S. Oh no, for goodness'sake.

FERNAND. It was just to make you laugh, that I said five
to nine, don't you see? What have I done to you?

MME S. Nothing at all. I'm going to put it back in the oven.
I'm going to put it back in the oven.

FERNAND. What's the matter with her? Oh look here, what's
the matter with her?

MME S. The matter with me? Well, I'll tell you what it is -
what the matter is - liar!

FERNAND. What? Liar? What what what?

MME S. What was it that was making you laugh, just now,
with that child?

FERNAND. You know as well as I do. The hat!

MME S. Liar!

FERNAND. It was. It was. It was. Poor little thing. You
saw her, though, with her little white dress, looking so
pathetic, so sad. So you see. We had a good laugh,
that's all.

MME S. Yes.

FERNAND. Well yes, of course! but... No no, really, you'd be making a mistake. It was like this: we were just facing each other, me with my hat on, and then... and then what? Nothing, nothing at all: we had a good laugh.

MME S. Then you can tell me what you're hiding in your hand.

FERNAND. In my hand?

MME S. Yes; since you came back.

FERNAND. Nothing; nothing at all. It's... it's a cork. Nothing, eh.

MME S. Show me.

FERNAND. I haven't the slightest reason to show you this cork.

MME S. Liar.

FERNAND. (Suddenly) All right, then - no! So there! It isn't a cork. It isn't even anything like a cork! Here! Look! Have a good look! Got it? Now do you know what it is?

MME S. What is it?

FERNAND. It's a lens! Precisely; a lens. That sets you back a bit, eh? Well, it doesn't worry me in the least.

MME S. Ah!

FERNAND. In the least.

MME S. Yes. Well, I... what d'you expect me to say? It doesn't worry me, either.

FERNAND. (After a pause) Yes. Well then. I'll screw it in again.

MME S. (After some slight confusion) What shall we do?

102

Shall we eat it?

FERNAND. Yes, oh...

MME S. Oh... (She puts the tart down and seems exhausted) ... I don't know. I don't know what I'm doing, I don't know what I'm saying. I don't know what you're saying, or what you're doing. Oh... Look here, eh, what's the matter? What's the matter, Bertrand? Go on, go on, Bertrand...

FERNAND. I'm not here. If you call me Bertrand, he's not here.

MME S. Yes, well, it comes to the same thing. What's the matter with you, Fernand?

FERNAND. I've got a lens to screw in.

MME S. Screw it in then. What's the matter, Fernand? Don't you love me any more?

FERNAND. I can't do two things at once! Screw in a lens and love you, Madame!

MME S. Bertrand!

FERNAND. And then, the thing that's really the matter with me is that my name isn't Bertrand. Even when I'm screwing in a lens, Madame!

MME S. Don't call me Madame!

FERNAND. Don't call me Bertrand!

(MADAME SÉVERIN collapses, in tears)

Auntie... are you crazy? What is it, eh? Now what's the matter? Do you want me to go and fetch you another bottle of aspirin? with a big glass of water? From Switzerland?

MME S. No.

FERNAND. Well then!.... You know very well it's all finished.

MME S. The water? Isn't there any more water?

FERNAND. What! Are you still thirsty?

MME S. Oh, thirsty!....

FERNAND. Well then, all you have to do is not cry, my dear. Crying dries you up...

MME S. You're all I've got, now...

FERNAND. That's not much, I'll admit.

(A second or two of the sound of the electric machine)

MME S. She's calling you.

FERNAND. Yes, I...

MME S. Go on, then; go on.

FERNAND. Oh yes! Like hell I'm going to put myself out! Little bitches. They're all the same. Just like Germaine, eh. Her dress, oh no, she's not interested in it any more, you don't really think she'll come and fetch it, do you? They go around showing their behinds to all and sundry, you don't need anything else for a motor bike, after all.

MME S. Don't say that, Fernand.

FERNAND. After all we've done for her.

MME S. You say that because you didn't know her when she was little.

FERNAND. Did you?

MME S. I didn't either. But I did Bertrand.

FERNAND. A disgusting fellow, that Bertrand.

104

MME S. You wouldn't say that if you'd known him when he was so high. He was so blond.

FERNAND. So blond!

MME S. Yes, and he had two little legs. He was so sweet. So very sweet. He looked like a celluloid baby. Especially in the water. And then, he ran so fast! You'd lose sight of him, you'd call, and back he'd come, you'd see him at the far end of the path, looking even smaller, just a little speck on the horizon, but he already had great big eyes that looked at you. I used to say to him: Bertrand, your eyes are bigger than your stomach, but no! The moment you put his plate in front of him it was empty, and he wasn't fussy. He adored bread and milk. He'd gulp down his bread and milk and laugh like anything! and he was so popular. People used to say to him: Bertrand, it's not nice, chasing little girls like that and giving them ideas, and he'd answer: I like my bread and milk better. He was a child in a million, and such a soft heart! His heart was bigger than he was. He'd got everything. The day of his first communion he collected all the old candle ends from the church and gave them to his cousin Yvette; the priest was furious! And later on, too, when he'd got that little Solange in my bed with him, one evening when he didn't expect me back because the trains were on strike, he told Solange to go away and he begged my pardon. It made me cry. It made Solange cry, too. But of course, at that age, he didn't cry any more.

FERNAND. Solange, ah yes; now there was a girl who liked motor bikes.

MME S. Oh, you!

FERNAND. Yes. She liked motor bikes all right, that girl did.

MME S. Nothing but motor bikes. Anyone might think that's all that matters to you, motor bikes.

FERNAND. And when I say: motor bikes, I mean by herself, you know what I mean? Not on the pillion. Ha! You

ought to have seen her! like this: Prrrrr... A real little
woman. And she knew all about the way they worked, and
everything. That's how we met her, anyway, me and
Bertrand. I can just see myself, I was smoking my cigar,
after lunch it was, I was in the side, he was on the car,
and it was going like hell, Bertrand's side car, it wasn't
a toy, you know. We were doing a good 80! All of a
sudden, what do we see? Ha! my dear girl! there's a
hell of a screech - Bertrand's jamming on his brakes.
Solange is on the side of the road, her motor bike's
lying on the grass, and she's cleaning her jet! We were
absolutely flabbergasted. And all her plugs scattered
around in the greenery, like a fireworks display. So
it won't surprise you to hear that we took her in tow.
No, but really, joking apart, she was a rare bird,
Solange. And so sweet, so charming, with it all, and
not very tall; the mixed strawberry and vanilla cornet
type, luscious, a real dish! But of course! that's what
we need - Solange!

MME S. Solange?

FERNAND. To model for the photos. If Germaine doesn't
    come back.

MME S. What d'you mean: if Germaine doesn't come back?

FERNAND. Oh no, because... Madame Séverin, modelling,
    that wouldn't be a job for you.

MME S. Eh? What?...

FERNAND. Oh no; you'll see. Hats, fine, but photography
    no, from the publicity point of view, it just doesn't pay.

MME S. Photos! Motor bikes! Photos! What do they matter
    to me!

FERNAND. Of course! Photos aren't you, motor bikes
    aren't you - but hats are.

MME S. Solange, Solange! She can take her photos, and her
    motor bikes, anywhere she likes, but she's not going to
    set foot here any more!

FERNAND. All right all right... but even so, you won't be the one to replace Germaine.

MME S. Germaine!

FERNAND. Well, with me, it's all right once, yes, but...

MME S. But who ever told you that Germaine wouldn't come back?

FERNAND. How d'you mean: who? She did.

MME S. She did? But she was here a week ago. Why shouldn't she come today? Seeing that it's Sunday! And there's a cheese tart!

FERNAND. Because she didn't tell you she'd come.

MME S. Germaine?

FERNAND. Nor did Bertrand.

MME S. Germaine didn't tell me she wouldn't come.

FERNAND. What did she tell you, then?

MME S. Nothing!

FERNAND. Nothing!

MME S. Nothing!

FERNAND. Well, if that's all you need, me too, I'll say nothing. In any case, I've already said it.

MME S. Germaine would have told me. She's a good girl, Germaine.

FERNAND. Oh well! for that matter! Your little niece too, oh, what's her name now... Yvette too, she was a good girl... so what it comes to...

MME S. Naturally! Everyone can't be called Solange.

FERNAND. Oh, that... (He concentrates on opening another bottle)

MME S. Drunkard!

FERNAND. Of course. When I think of Bertrand, well, really! With his motor bike! and that the only thing he ever gets excited about, that boy, isn't just the motor of his motor bike, but the motors of all motor bikes in general, not forgetting aeroplane motors! And that that girl, that little thingummy, what's her name again? Germaine! I tried to explain the principle of the two-stroke engine to her - there's absolutely nothing to it! ... Bah! Yes - it wasn't even that she didn't understand: but that she yawned. Well then, just imagine them, the two of them, in Pontoise, in a garage, up to their ears in grease, and her yawning! yawning! when the slightest little pinprick knocks all the stuffing out of him, his morale being what it is! Ha! I can just imagine them! Oh yes! She's certainly just the girl he needed, old Bertrand.

MME S. And what about her? Do you think he's just the boy she needed?

FERNAND. She? She's yawning! and so...

MME S. She's yawning! Well, that just proves how much she's enjoying herself! In Pontoise, in a garage, up to her ears in grease, poor little thing! And I've never seen a girl so gifted for making hats.

FERNAND. Hats!

MME S. Ladies' hats, of course. Because to make something to go on a head like yours, you'd really have to have vicious tendencies.

FERNAND. So I should imagine! but you needn't worry! You can keep your old hats, so far as we are concerned; we lose our hair and go bald - we think that looks nicer.

MME S. Nicer!

FERNAND. And less pathetic.

MME S. Pathetic! My hats, pathetic! and your bikes, they aren't pathetic, I suppose?

FERNAND. They go pop pop...

MME S. Poppycock! You poor crackpots! Going pop pop isn't pathetic, perhaps? You're potty! Ptt...

FERNAND. And then they start to operate...

MME S. Ptt! You're pathological! They start to operate! Yes, with you in front, you poor peasants, and us patriarchs parking our fannies in the poop, it's all the same to you, they start to operate! but they don't get anywhere.

FERNAND. They don't get anywhere!...

MME S. Well, in any case, Bertrand's didn't get anywhere.

FERNAND. Oh look here, really!

MME S. I can just see them the two of them - look! crushed against a tree-trunk, their motor bike on top of them in the branches.

FERNAND. Oh no, oh look here, all the same, Auntie, don't pile it on.

MME S. I know we mustn't hope for the worst...

FERNAND. Oh!... No!...

MME S. But she got off on the wrong foot, that poor child.

FERNAND. She shouldn't have gone off on either foot; that's all. (To the corkscrew) What the hell's the matter with you?

MME S. And that's why I say she'll come back.

FERNAND. She'll come back?

MME S. Of course she will. In any case, we can't even say

she's gone, as she was here a week ago, and she certainly won't be long now.

FERNAND. Yes but, yes but, yes but...

MME S. What?

FERNAND. What's the matter with this corkscrew?

MME S. Oh! it's Emile's old corkscrew.

FERNAND. Yes, but...

MME S. You shouldn't have used that one.

(And in fact, as he turns the handle, the horizontal bits
of the corkscrew descend, but the spiral sticks in the
top of the cork and doesn't budge)

FERNAND. ... in the meantime, I damn nearly punctured
my hand.

MME S. Y'ought to've used the other one... here.

FERNAND. Yes, all very funny; better not happen again.
She'll come back! sure! but she'd better not come back
too often.

MME S. She'll come back!... I'm talking about Germaine.

FERNAND. In that case, you shouldn't have slung her out.

MME S. What? me?

FERNAND. Yes, you.

MME S. She went because Bertrand did.

FERNAND. Yes, but who slung Bertrand out?

MME S. He did: he slung himself out.

FERNAND. Should've stopped him.

MME S. Him? Bertrand! But what d'you expect me to do with him - with Bertrand?

FERNAND. That poor little boy, so blond, he was, who used to run round the park demanding his bread and milk.

MME S. Oh yes, of course, eh; but it was some little time since he'd been demanding his bread and milk.

FERNAND. You wouldn't have given it to him! At his age, after he'd been running round the park calling for his bread and milk for twenty years, it was time he shut up a bit. He might even have hoped that he didn't need to yell any more for someone to give him his bread and milk.

MME S. At his age you don't ask for your bread and milk any more; you take it!

FERNAND. Right; so he said to himself: good night, all, I'm going to get my bread and milk elsewhere. And he went.

MME S. Well - best thing he could have done. Only he didn't need to take that child with him.

FERNAND. She didn't need to let herself be taken. That's what I say: they've gone.

MME S. Of course not; of course they haven't gone. People don't just go like that, without telling anyone! People don't go like that without knowing the place.

FERNAND. The place: Ah, my poor Auntie! it's quite obvious you don't know what a place is! But there are places everywhere! You can't take a step without putting your foot on one. Just look around you, you poor dear. On your right, on your left, down there, up in the air, behind the screens, everywhere, you'll see places.

MME S. Yes, but there's good ones and bad ones.

FERNAND. But you get used to the bad ones! Take this shop, for example, haven't I got used to it? And in less than

111

no time.

MME S. Naturally! When you find yourself in a shop! So I
should think! But what if you'd found yourself somewhere
else! in the soup, for instance, well, people don't get
used to that in less than no time.

FERNAND. It'd have taken me longer, that's all. And there's
no shortage of time, there's always plenty of that, it's
like places. And what's more, it doesn't cost anything.

MME S. Time? But you still have to pay for what you pass it
with. Time doesn't feed you.

FERNAND. Oh, go on, feeding yourself isn't difficult - you
just eat. You eat, and that's all there is to it.

MME S. You eat what?

FERNAND. Whatever there happens to be. I dunno. A
cheese tart.

MME S. If you want to eat a cheese tart you have to go to a
place where there is a cheese tart.

FERNAND. There are cheese tarts everywhere.

MME S. There aren't, you know.

FERNAND. Well - everywhere where there's cheese, of
course.

MME S. And where there are tarts, too. Look here, they
can't have gone far. They'll be back.

FERNAND. I don't say they won't.

MME S. They'll be back.

FERNAND. I don't say they won't.

MME S. They'll be back.

FERNAND. Fat lot of good it'll do them. (In the meantime,

he has poured out the vermouth) Here: your health! And us too; fat lot of good it'll do us. Let them go away, though! Let them go away to some places! Let them eat their grease tart! I don't need it. What? Do you need it, Auntie - their grease tart?

MME S. You only think of yourself.

FERNAND. They can have it, since they're so fond of it, since they enjoy it, since they're the right age for it. Mustn't force them. You're the one that only thinks of herself.

MME S. I am? I was thinking of myself, I suppose, when I said to myself: I know, I'll make a cheese tart this afternoon!

FERNAND. Oh, I know very well you weren't thinking of yourself. You weren't thinking of me either, though.

MME S. Not of you, not of you...

FERNAND. Oh come now, I'm only too well aware of it! - that I don't count for very much with you.

MME S. Oh Fernand, you always say the same thing.

FERNAND. Because it's true. And anyway, it's all my fault.

MME S. Listen! there they are!

FERNAND. Where?

MME S. The motor bike.

FERNAND. What? It isn't, you know, it's the girl next door grinding her coffee.

MME S. (Drinking) This is good; what is it?

FERNAND. I don't know. Bleach.

MME S. Bleach! Ha! do you remember?

FERNAND. Of course I do.

MME S. What a laugh we had! - do you remember - I was
sitting there, Germaine was here, Bertrand was over
there, and you... where on earth were you, now?

FERNAND. Here. But it's not true, we weren't laughing
as much as all that. You know, though, I'd quite like
to invite Duchenard, now, but you don't like him. And
anyway, it's a fact, he's been less amusing recently,
old Duchenard. And then I must admit that Duchenard,
he probably doesn't realize it, but he's getting to
smell worse and worse. In fact, Duchenard stinks.
There'd certainly be...

MME S. She wouldn't want to.

FERNAND. That... well, that's another matter. But what
would we do with him?

MME S. Quite!

FERNAND. Well then? (He pours himself out a drink) What
d'you want me to do?

MME S. Why, nothing, Fernand! Who's asking you to do
anything?

FERNAND. No one. Oh, that! I've nothing to worry about
on that score. No one asks me to do anything any more.

MME S. Well then...

FERNAND. No one needs me, what. (He fills MADAME
SÉVERIN's glass)

MME S. No one needs you! But what would I do without you?
Who'd go and buy my pins and muslin for me? And my
velvets, my espartos, my straws and my felts, and that
big crate of trimmings over there, with feathers,
flowers and ribbons, that you brought me yesterday,
on your back! Who'd take care of all that if you didn't,
Fernand? But I couldn't do without you, now!

FERNAND. (Who doesn't think this is a very good joke) Yes, oh yes! of course.

MME S. Come on, come on, come on, what's the matter with my pet, eh? There, he's going to tell his little Auntie all about it, right? (She goes and sits on his knees) Isn't he? But I don't think he looks very healthy. And just see how thin he is.

FERNAND. Mind my glass.

MME S. You drink too much. We don't need to look any further than that. And then, you don't eat.

FERNAND. I don't eat! I don't eat all the time, no!

MME S. Listen.

FERNAND. Yes.

MME S. Listen, listen little Fernand. You know the tart, the nice cheese tart?

FERNAND. Yes.

MME S. What would you say if we started on it, without them?

FERNAND. The cheese tart?

MME S. Ah, you are just a little bit interested in it, aren't you, my pet...

FERNAND. You're hurting my knee.

MME S. Kiss me.

FERNAND. How'll I cut it? in two?

MME S. Just a little kiss first.

FERNAND. My glass, for the love of mike! No but what are you after, eh? What d'you want? What?

MME S. Me?

FERNAND. Owch! my knee...

MME S. Oh all right all right, very well. (She gets up and sits in her chair again) When you're trying to be nice to someone...

FERNAND. Oh! So you're being nice to me! What more could I want! I'll be delighted to eat your cheese tart. But that's no reason to dislocate my knee... Well, shall I cut it in two?

MME S. Oh no, even so. We must leave them a bit, just in case they come.

FERNAND. Oh, really! In any case, I know what I'm going to do. We're not the right age for all this any more. Oh hell!

MME S. What?

FERNAND. There they are.

MME S. No they're not. It's the little girl next door washing her hair.

FERNAND. Are you sure?

MME S. Of course I am.

FERNAND. Doesn't usually make so much noise when she washes her hair.

MME S. No, nor she does, you're right, it's the...

FERNAND. Of course. A little vermouth, first.

MME S. ... the central heating switching itself on.

FERNAND. Come on, have a drink, it'll cheer you up. And anyway, the central heating isn't working.

MME S. You drink too much. You're drinking more and more.

116

FERNAND. Got to keep warm somehow. Help yourself.

MME S. We're not the right age! If Germaine was here I know very well you wouldn't say you weren't the right age any more.

FERNAND. Because she is the right age... Come on, let's finish the tart, because if they don't come I'm going back to my thingummy...

MME S. Oh yes! Just leave me flat!

(A pause. They don't move. MADAME SÉVERIN is listening to what might be a motor bike, and FERNAND is watching the fly)

FERNAND. Look! The fly's back. Ah, so you smelt the cheese, did you? You see, it understands every word!

MME S. Yerss, yerss... A fly.

FERNAND. Oh yes, of course ! What's a fly? We're so much more intelligent, we've got so many more important things in our heads, I suppose!

MME S. Oh, speak for yourself, Fernand! If you only knew how stupid and insignificant I feel!

FERNAND. Not now!

MME S. But Fernand, that fly, if I met it in the street, I'd be the first to say hallo!

FERNAND. (To the fly) Not over there, not over there!

MME S. Yes but, if I still have enough energy to make a tart on a Sunday afternoon, and then I see it's only a fly that's interested in it, it makes me sad.

FERNAND. A fly, a fly, eh! A fly and me, at least. (He blows on the fly, which flies away)

MME S. And then - if I could only be sure my tart was going to be good.

FERNAND. Of course it will be - here! (He takes a bite)

MME S. Eatable, is it?

FERNAND. (Realizing that it isn't) ... Try it.

MME S. What's the matter?

FERNAND. Well, there's certainly some cheese in your tart. But there's certainly some soap, too.

MME S. Soap! Two big bits of gruyère I put in it!

FERNAND. One piece of gruyère, yes. And the piece of soap that was in the cupboard next to the gruyère. (A pause) It's my fault.

(He gets up. An alarm clock rings)

MME S. I thought you'd found someone who was going to buy all those things?

FERNAND. I had, but in the end he didn't want to.

MME S. They go all right, though.

FERNAND. Yes, but not at the same speed.

MME S. Almost.

FERNAND. And anyway, he was a collector. These aren't collector's clocks.

MME S. All the same, we'll have to get rid of them. I'd quite like to be able to use the hammock.

FERNAND. (Has opened the screens, and taken from behind them an enormous china vase, shapeless and unfinished) It's up to the two of us, now.

MME S. Huh! Isn't it broken yet?

FERNAND. It's beginning to look nice, don't you think?

MME S. And how far is it going to come up to, your vase?

FERNAND. Dunno. (He starts sticking the vase together, and whistling 'Simple swallows. ')

(MADAME SÉVERIN gives him a bored look)

OTHER C AND B PLAYSCRIPTS

* PS 1   TOM PAINE
Paul Foster

* PS 2   BALLS and other plays
(The Recluse, Hurrah for the Bridge, The Hessian
Corporal)
Paul Foster

   PS 3   THREE PLAYS
(Coda, Lunchtime Concert, The Inhabitants)
Olwen Wymark

* PS 4   CLEARWAY
Vivienne C. Welburn

* PS 5   JOHNNY SO LONG and THE DRAG
Vivienne C. Welburn

* PS 6   SAINT HONEY and OH DAVID, ARE YOU THERE?
Paul Ritchie

   PS 7   WHY BOURNEMOUTH? and other plays
(The Missing Links, An Apple a Day)
John Antrobus

* PS 8   THE CARD INDEX and other plays
(The Interrupted Act, Gone Out)
Tadeusz Rozewicz
tr. Adam Czerniawski

   PS 9   US
Peter Brook and others

* PS 10   SILENCE and THE LIE
Nathalie Sarraute
tr. Maria Jolas

* PS 11   THE WITNESSES and other plays
(The Laocoon Group, The Funny Old Man)
Tadeusz Rozewicz
tr. Adam Czerniawski

* PS 12   THE CENCI
Antonin Artaud
tr. Simon Watson-Taylor

* PS 13   PRINCESS IVONA
Witold Gombrowicz
tr. Krystyna Griffith-Jones and Catherine Robins

* All plays marked with an asterisk are represented for
  dramatic presentation by C and B (Theatre) Limited
  18 Brewer Street London W1R 4AS